Without hesitation, Giles fought his way into the leaping, cutting pillar of dust, searching for Petia. His lips thinned to a line; he dared not let the sand fill his mouth and choke him. Blindly, he flailed about seeking her. Red agony burned in his veins now. The bone goggles he wore blinded him in the darkness of the djinn's mischief and did little to hold back the dust.

He fought against the buffeting winds—and he found her. Giles almost fell over the writhing woman but managed to keep his balance. He grabbed Petia's shoulders and assisted her to her feet. When she was standing, he put one arm around her waist and drew his sword, awkwardly thumbing the inscription and feeling the blaze of energy. The enemy might be only a mass of swirling dust, but his anger knew no bounds. If the power of the sword allowed them to fight their way out, he'd use it!

Barely had he leveled the sword when a corridor through the shroud of brown opened before them. Giles held the sword before him and half carried Petia to the perimeter of the dust storm. As they cleared the edge of the whirlwind and stumbled into the hot desert sun, Giles swung his blade mightily at the axis of the vortex. He heard a howl from the miniature tornado's core. The whirling dust stilled and fell to the desert floor, revealing an immense djinn in human guise.

The desert was quiet once more.

THE SKELETON
LORD'S KEY

Tor books by Robert Vardeman writing as Daniel Moran

THE FLAME KEY
THE SKELETON LORD'S KEY

KEYS TO PARADISE

BOOK II

THE SKELETON LORD'S KEY

ROBERT E. VARDEMAN
writing as
DANIEL MORAN

TOR

A TOM DOHERTY ASSOCIATES BOOK

THE SKELETON LORD'S KEY

Copyright © 1987 by Daniel Moran

First printing: August 1987

A TOR Book

Published by Tom Doherty Associates, Inc.
49 West 24 Street
New York, N.Y. 10010

Cover art by Judith Mitchell

ISBN: 0-812-54602-4
CAN. ED.: 0-812-54603-2

Printed in the United States of America

0 9 8 7 6 5 4 3 2 1

To Tim, Sean, and Shannon—
Scattered but still together

Chapter One

"There's no honor among thieves, and you two are thieves by trade. How else do you expect me to react?"

Giles Grimsmate studied his two companions. They averted their eyes and didn't return his hard look. Keja Tchurak seldom looked Giles in the eye when speaking. The grizzled old veteran had come to expect nothing but subterfuge and excuses from the light-fingered, fair-haired Keja. But from the cat-Trans he expected more. Petia Darya lacked Keja's long years of experience at filching anything not securely guarded, but she more than made up for it with earnest ambition to be like him.

Such a pair they were, Giles reflected. The old man shook his head. How they had come together in this mad scheme seemed almost a dream to him—or was it a nightmare? After returning from the Trans War, all he'd wanted to do was find a bit of solace in his old village. That had lasted only a few short months. The village had changed; Giles had changed even more. Not for the first time he cursed his craving for action, for just one more grand adventure before dying. Then he cursed Keja and Petia for holding out such hope to him. Hope was for the young, not the old and cynical.

Still, life was not so bad at the moment, Giles decided. The three rode sturdy horses that Petia had acquired in Dimly New. The morning sky was resplendent as the sun glanced off feathery ice clouds and cast down on the world a shower of warmth and promise. Giles couldn't even complain about his arthritic joints since the sun soaked up moisture from the night's shower. The land sparkled and the day was off to a fine start—except for the argument.

Keja looked up, brushed back a lock of hair with a quick, nervous gesture and said, "Look, Giles. After all we've been

1

through, I don't know why you don't trust us. Petia nursed you after our escape from the cave. We could have stolen your key then and left you to die in the woods."

"I've wondered about that," Giles said. "But I think you draw a line between taking people's property and people's lives. I'll grant you this, you've done your share in keeping me alive and getting us out of Dimly New. But now that I've healed, I think my key is fair game again." Giles saw Keja trying to look innocent. A hunting eagle had a better chance of convincing a rabbit that it wasn't hungry. "I don't believe you trust each other, either."

They rode in glum, suspicious silence. The argument had begun immediately after they had escaped from Dimly New. In a few short days, the three had overturned a cult led by the Flame Sorceress, flooded her cavern stronghold, drowning the woman and most of her followers, and found the third key to the Gate of Paradise.

The search for the keys had thrown them together, and the possession of the keys now threatened their tenuous alliance. Giles had won his in a dice game. Keja had stolen his from a lover's father. Petia now held the third key wrested from the Flame Sorceress.

"Look," Giles said, "if we're going on with this crack-brained quest, we'd better make a decision right now. Three keys don't get us any closer to opening the Gate of Paradise than one did." When Giles and Keja had first attempted to open the legendary Gate, they had discovered five keys were required. It had been then that they decided to join forces and retrieve the remaining keys. Giles felt a pang of guilt at deceiving the others. Only he had deciphered the glyphs stating: Only One May Enter.

"I don't think we should keep the keys with us," Giles went on, seeing how his companions took his lack of trust in their integrity. "We could lose one or more of them, or have them stolen. Who knows what might happen to them? They'd be a lot safer left here."

"How do we know that?" Petia threw a dark glance at Giles. This day her cat nature had come to the forefront. Her eyes slitted like a feline's, and she made unconscious preening gestures over nonexistent whiskers. The product of magicks and spells long since forgotten, the Trans combined human and animal traits—and had provoked a war over their lack of status. Giles liked Petia well enough as a person, but had little time for any Trans even though he'd fought against their enslavement. Too many bitter years of his life had been wasted, too many lives lost, too many of his family killed.

"You must not know anything about mercantile houses." The Trans indicated that she didn't.

"They act as clearing houses for the commerce of many countries. They are the banks for commercial accounts. And they are safer than any other place I know to leave valuable properties. They have excellent reputations that they work hard to keep. If you two don't want to leave your keys safely in Sanustell, I'll just say good-bye and be on my way. I don't think I'd care to go on. Or you can make me an offer for my key."

Petia and Keja both turned in their saddles and stared at Giles in astonishment. "You don't mean that, do you?"

"I do. I don't feel like waking up someday to find myself abandoned and my key missing. Either we put the keys in safekeeping or I'm off."

Silence descended again like a heavy, cloaking fog. Giles had made his final statement. He was tired to the center of his soul. His shoulder still ached from the flaming arrow the sorceress had flung at him, and he didn't care whether he continued on or not. Foolhardy quests were not his style when the lovely city of Sanustell offered so many immediate comforts for an ancient warrior.

Sunlight played on the high walls of Sanustell. Morning traffic streamed through the gates. Patiently the three joined the line and passed into the city, receiving only a slight nod from the guard.

"Where are we going to stay?" Petia asked.

"I don't care where you stay," Giles answered. He had received no answer from Keja or Petia and presumed they were finished with him. "I'm going to find an inn, have a bath and a good meal, and spend the evening drinking, in hopes that I'll sleep well."

"What do you mean you don't care where we stay?" Keja asked, aggrieved.

"Just that. You obviously don't want to give up the keys,

so I'm finished with it. You're on your own. It's been a pleasure knowing you."

"Wait, Giles! You can't go off like this."

Giles had already turned his horse and headed across the square toward an alley that led toward the quarter of the city where the inns clustered. He waved tiredly without looking back.

Petia and Keja stared at each other. "What do you think?" she asked.

Keja shrugged. "I think we need him. It galls me to say that. It is even worse admitting that we'd better give in."

They trotted after the disappearing man.

The stately room radiated warmth from the rich wood tones of the ironbeam. Candles cast their glow along the paneling, and a polished table of the same wood dominated the center of the room. Silver candelabra held candles of pure beeswax to light transactions made here.

The door at one end of the room opened and a man made his grand entrance as befitting a member of the mercantile elite.

He was slender, and though his clothes were cut stylishly, they were of a somber gray. He paused for a moment, examining his would-be clients. "Welcome to Callant Hanse," he said, as if coming to a conclusion of vast importance, and strode down the length of the room to take his place at the head of the table.

"I am Simon Callant. What may I do for you?"

Giles sat back in his chair and waited for the others to answer for him. He was so tired. When no one responded, he roused himself and looked at Petia and Keja.

"You tell him, Giles," Keja said. Petia nodded.

Giles sighed. Why couldn't someone else take the lead just once? Too worn to waste any time, Giles spoke. "We have three keys to the Gate of Paradise, which we wish to leave in your safekeeping."

"I see," Callant said with only a slightly raised eyebrow. "May I see them?"

The three reached inside their tunics, and each pulled forth a string. From each cord dangled a golden key.

Giles handed his to Callant. He watched as the man

examined it. He was amused as the banker's eyebrows arched higher with each passing second.

"Amazing," Callant whispered. "Is this truly the key to the Gate of Paradise? I've heard the legend, of course, but never dreamed that there was any truth to it."

"*A* key to the Gate of Paradise," Giles corrected. "That key opens only one lock. There are five on the Gate. And this is one legend with more than a hint of truth to it. We know that to be true."

"You wish Callant Hanse to safeguard the keys?"

"Yes. We have two more keys to collect and we"—he glanced at Keja and Petia—"*I* thought it would be best if we left them. We don't wish to risk losing what we have gained."

"No doubt." Simon Callant rose and shook a bell pull. A servant silently entered with wine and cheese. "Please help yourselves."

Keja didn't need a second invitation, not having eaten since the night before. Petia poured small glasses of a rich, red wine. Giles declined the food but took the wine, sipping it in appreciation. Callant Hanse did not serve the swill he usually got at inns.

"Would you tell me how you came by these keys?" Callant asked.

"I think not," Giles said. "I thought it was a policy of your hanse not to ask questions."

"My apologies," he said. "It's just that I was so fascinated by your story that I allowed curiosity to best me." Giles wondered at that. Simon Callant did not appear to be a man who ever let emotion rule him. "The keys to the Gate of Paradise. Imagine that. But you are absolutely right. We do not ask questions. There is one thing I must know, however, before we can agree to this commission. You say that you search for the final two keys to the Gate. What is Callant Hanse to do with the keys if you do not return for them? I presume that there is a certain amount of danger in such a venture."

"No need to worry about that," Keja said, his mouth full of thin wheat flatbread. "We will return."

"And if you don't?" Callant persisted. "The house must know your wishes if these keys are not claimed."

"All three of us must claim the keys—or none gets them," Giles said. "Is there something we must sign?" Both Petia and Keja started to protest, but the cold look Giles shot them kept them silent.

Callant saw that the ex-soldier did not wish to waste any more time. He summoned the house scribe who, within seconds, was seated with his pen poised and ready to write.

The form was simple and quickly done. All three signed. When Callant had affixed his signature as witness and chop as officer of the hanse, he held out his hand for the keys.

Reluctantly, Keja and Petia handed them over.

"Remember," Callant said. "All three of you must be present when you wish to collect these keys."

"You're certain they will be safe here?" Keja asked, still unsure of what he'd just done.

"We have never had anything stolen or missing from our care," Simon Callant said haughtily. "They will be locked in a strongbox and kept in a room guarded at all times. You have nothing to fear."

Giles rose wearily from the table and motioned the others toward the door. "We thank you for your assistance. I am sure we will all sleep the better knowing the keys are safe."

"Would it be possible to see where—" Keja cut short his question when he saw the look in Giles' eye. "No, I suppose not." He turned for the door.

"I thought you hated water," Keja said to Petia. "You've been extolling the luxuries of that hot bath for the last half hour."

"There's a difference between icy cold mountain water coming up around your neck and threatening to drown you and hot, steamy bath water you sink down to your neck in and inhale the fine, subtle fragrance of beldon leaves." Petia sipped from her glass of light, golden wine, swallowed and smiled wickedly at Keja.

"If I recall rightly," she added, "wasn't it you who perched atop a rocky outcropping like some gargoyle? You don't swim at all and must hate water as much as I do, so don't tell me you didn't enjoy a hot bath, too."

Keja laughed. "You're right. Cold water from a mountain stream; there's nothing better to drink. And a hot bath, yes.

But I was terrified in the cave," he said in a low voice. "Thank the gods for Giles."

"That's not what you were saying a few hours ago."

Petia and Keja looked up at the sound of Giles' voice. Keja pulled a chair up to the table, gesturing to it.

Giles sat and motioned to a serving maid. His hair still dripped from his bath. He wiped perspiration from his forehead. "Maybe that bath will sweat some of the poisons out of this old body. We used to do that back when I was soldiering. A kind of sweat bath that the men from the north country said was common to their people."

The maid brought a goblet filled with the golden wine.

"What next, Giles?" Keja made small, wet circles on the table with the base of his goblet.

Giles shook his head. "I don't want to think about it. Let's not even talk about it. Let's enjoy a dinner and then while away the evening with drink and good talk. Talk about anything but those thrice-damned keys, where they are, and how to get them. All right?"

"I just thought . . ."

Petia reached out and laid a finger on Keja's wrist. She shook her head and mouthed "no" at him.

All fell silent, wrapped in their own thoughts. Perhaps Giles did not want to talk about the keys, but the subject occupied all three minds. Finally Giles stirred. He tipped his empty goblet, and Petia filled it again for him.

"Have you found out what there is for dinner?" Giles asked.

"Too busy drinking," Keja said.

"Well, let's dine, shall we? I'm starved. And I don't care what they charge. I'm eating till I've doubled my waistline!"

The meal was sumptuous. The first course was a thick stew of seafoods containing crab, mussels, a local white bottom fish and potatoes, served with loaves of brown bread direct from the ovens. Thick slabs of meat followed, cut from a roast hindquarter of delaine ox, which had been turning on a spit since morning. A bread pudding laced with dried hurryberries and spiced delicately with casticon finished the meal off.

Giles ate everything on the plate before him and finished off by asking for a second helping of the dessert, with a double portion of thick cream poured over it.

Conversation ceased during the meal. When the dishes were cleared, Giles asked for brandy. He filled his pipe and lighted it, puffing silently, nearly hidden in the wreaths of pungent blue smoke around his head.

Keja and Petia made small talk and left Giles to his own thoughts. Petia watched the other people in the room, interested in the clientele attracted by this inn. She watched a dark man dressed in black seat himself at the table behind Keja and Giles. He turned his head to eavesdrop every time that she or Keja said anything. She had never seen him before, but the Trans dismissed him out of hand. City people always enjoyed spying on their neighbors.

The brandy finally loosened Giles' tongue. He talked about his life, his war years, the family he had lost. Petia sensed somehow that he needed to get it all out. She prodded him when he slowed, poured more brandy when he emptied his glass.

Three pipes and six glasses later, Giles had told his story and was nodding. "We'd better get him up to bed," Petia said.

Keja managed to get Giles on his feet.

"Careful with his shoulder," Petia cautioned.

They made it up the stairway without falling over the banister and got him onto the bed. "That's all he gets," Petia said. She felt none too steady herself. They threw a blanket over Giles and left.

"Petia?" Keja said softly. "The nights have been long —and lonely. Would you share my bed tonight?" The small thief's eyes gleamed with an inner light that was more feral than human.

For all they meant to each other as comrades in arms, Petia wanted nothing to do with Keja as a lover. Better Giles.

She swallowed and rubbed one hand across her forehead. Too much brandy, she decided, to ever think such a thing. She was Trans; Giles was human. There were laws. Besides, he was more of a father to her. Yes, a father.

"You remember what I said to you last time you asked that? The answer hasn't changed. You sleep alone tonight, though there may come a day. But don't whistle until it happens, or you'll wear out your lips puckering." Petia turned, lost her balance and put her hand on the wall to catch herself. Then she straightened and staggered down the hall to her room.

Keja remained standing, looking dolefully after her. "Good night, cat lady," he whispered with more feeling than was his wont.

The night was colder than Petia had anticipated. She pulled her cloak more closely about her shoulders and tried to balance on the gable. Her foot slipped and she barely caught herself.

She looked out across the city, trying to find a route across the rooftops, but did not see an obvious one. Sighing, she decided she would be better off on the ground. Once in the street, she backed away from the building, memorizing it so she would recognize it when she returned.

Petia closed her eyes and let the part of her that was cat take ascendancy, then made her way across the eastern quarter of the city until she reached Callant Hanse. She stood quietly in the deep shadows, watching the square and the building for any sign of activity. There was none.

She edged cautiously around the square until she stood beneath the elegant gold-chased sign that read simply CALLANT HANSE. She saw no easy access to its roof. A balcony extended outward at the third level, but otherwise the building displayed a distressingly plain front.

Changing tactics Petia scouted the back of the building. From there she could see light inside the building. The guard, of course, wouldn't stand watch in the dark. She purred without even realizing it. What a good idea! They should hire cat-Trans who could see in the dark. Like her.

She crept toward the adjoining building and swung up onto a loading dock. From there she gripped a windowsill and pulled herself up to a lip that protruded only inches out from a double door. A projecting beam for pulleys was the last step onto the roof.

After crossing swiftly to the hanse, she made her way to the front, then stepped down easily to the balcony. Once there, she hunched over, quietly catching her breath.

Petia faced a double door. She slid the blade of her knife

into the slight space where the two halves joined, then lifted it upward until the knife encountered metal. She exerted her strength and felt the metal bar give. Carefully she lifted it only far enough to be out of its catch, not wanting it to swing free and clatter. With her clawlike fingernails, she pulled one door outward.

The guard standing inside had his three-pronged spear at her throat in an instant. His comrade reached for her hands and clamped metal bracelets on them. A length of chain swung between.

Petia sobered at the ease with which they'd captured her. She should have known better than to try a burglary after drinking so much. Giles and Keja would be furious, and she could imagine the disapproving look on Simon Callant's ascetic face.

The guards dragged her down a hallway and threw her into a windowless room. She fell onto the wooden floor as the doors closed behind her. The key turned with grim finality.

The gray envelope was embossed with the Callant Hanse coat of arms. The note inside carried Simon Callant's chop. "At your earliest convenience," it read, "Callant Hanse requests the presence of Giles Grimsmate and Keja Tchurak."

"Should I wake Petia?" Keja asked.

"Let her sleep. Callant didn't ask for her, although I don't know why. Shall we be on our way?"

Keja quaffed the last of his breakfast ale, stuck a hard-boiled egg in his pocket and followed Giles out the door.

"I can't imagine what they want with us so early in the morning," Keja said. "I thought we took care of everything yesterday."

Giles snorted. "Probably some small detail, though Simon Callant didn't seem like a man to forget details, nor to admit it if he did."

The streets sparkled with early morning dew, but the day promised much. The sun slanted into dusty corners of the marketplace, and the place of the metal workers was already cloudy with smoke from their forges.

A servant awaited them at the door of Callant Hanse and

ushered them immediately to the room where they had met the previous day.

Simon Callant sat uneasily at the end of the table. Petia Darya stood between two guards to his side.

"What's this?" Giles cried angrily. His hand flashed to his sword.

Simon gestured for the Trans woman to explain.

Petia hung her head. "I'm sorry, Giles. I guess I'm rusty."

"You tried to burgle the keys?" Giles stood in open-mouthed surprise at this turn of events. His hand dropped away from his sword hilt.

Keja shook his head in dismay. "After what we've been through, you tried to get away with all three keys? Giles is right. We can't trust each other." He slumped into a chair. "You deserve a good whipping."

Callant broke in. "She deserves much more than that. If I turn her over to the city guard for attempted theft, she will be indentured for ten years. I nearly sent for the guard but thought that I should inform you first."

Giles looked at Callant. "Are you saying that it's up to us? We decide what happens to Petia?"

"Let me explain our position." Simon sipped from a cup of tea. "The Callant Hanse has a reputation to maintain. We are a trustworthy commercial concern of high standing. We would not like it known that a theft was even attempted here. We can send for the city guard and have her taken away. Or we can turn her over to you, and you may do with her as you like."

"Why should we want her?" Keja muttered.

"Yes, a good question." Giles looked at Callant for permission to help himself to the tea. He poured one for himself and one for Keja. "We have three keys, no thanks to Petia. We don't need a woman accompanying us whom we can't even trust. We'd be well rid of her. With all due respect, Callant, she is in your hands now. Your house is responsible. We might do well to leave her with you. The theft was attempted against you, not us."

"That's so. However," said Callant, "the agreement signed yesterday cannot be abrogated or abridged. If she is indentured, the keys remain in the possession of Callant Hanse until all three of you sign for them."

"There are some aspects of this woman's character which are attractive, however," Giles continued, seeing the difficulty pointed out by Callant. "We might consider them."

"The keys, lost," grumbled Keja. "Knew this was a bad idea."

Simon Callant sat back and listened to Giles and Keja debate Petia's fate, enjoying the Trans woman's embarrassment. He knew little about the strange relationship among the three and couldn't tell if the two men were being serious or not. If they arrived at a conclusion which would take her off his hands, he would be pleased. If not, he must proceed with formal charges.

"Perhaps we could allow her to work herself back into our good graces," Giles said.

Keja rubbed his hand alongside his face. "That's a possibility. There are some things she could do for us. At least I can think of one."

Petia grew more embarrassed—and angrier—with each passing comment.

Giles put down his cup and looked at Petia. "What do you have to say for yourself?"

"I say damn the both of you. If you don't care any more about me than that, I'll take indentures."

"You would. Callant, we will take Petia. We have our reasons, which we need not share with you. If your guards would unlock her bracelets, please."

As they left the room, Petia murmured, "I'll get even with you two for making me endure that."

Giles only shook his head, but Keja laughed loudly. Their lot had been cast. The keys—and each other—meant more to them than any cared admit aloud.

Chapter Two

"I don't know what we do now," Giles said. "We've spent all our money." He whittled a piece of wood away to nothing with his sharp dagger.

"We'll think of something," Keja said. "Something always blows our way, doesn't it, Petia?"

Petia sat in the corner with her back against the wall, knees drawn up and clasped in her arms, head down. She hadn't said a word since leaving Callant Hanse. The two men had embarrassed her. Chastened, she seethed. As much as she hated to admit it, they had been right; she was even angrier at herself for turning burglary into blundering.

Giles saw that she was feeling sorry for herself, but he had no sympathy for such petulance. It had been stupid trying to rob a well-guarded mercantile house.

"It's like the morning after the battle in here," Keja said. "Why don't we go to the marketplace?"

"Leave me alone."

"Come on, quit your sulking, Petia." He flung her cloak over her head, forcing her to come up for air. Then he grabbed Giles' jacket and his own and opened the door. "Let's go, you two. Fresh air and fresh outlooks are what you both need." He herded them down the stairs and out of the inn.

The marketplace sparkled in the sunshine. Vendors displayed their goods under brightly striped awnings, which shaded them from the sun and sheltered them from the rain that often swept in from the Everston Sea.

"I'm going to wander around," said Keja, "and see if any sterling opportunities arise." He flexed his fingers to show what he meant. "You have anything special you need me for, Giles?"

"No. We'll see you back at the inn."

13

"Yes, later." Keja waved and walked off into the crowd.

"I don't know the markets of Trois Havres," Giles said. "Is there likely to be a mapmaker or a dealer in maps?"

"There should be," Petia said listlessly. "Probably someone who doesn't deal exclusively in maps. Books and paper and such." She looked around and finally asked a fruit seller. With much arm waving, the merchant directed them to the far end of the marketplace.

They found a man sitting on a low stool, hands folded on his ample stomach, complacently watching the passing market-goers. Behind him were spread parchments, maps, illustrations, bound books, paper, pens and ink.

"Good day to you, sir and madam. What can I interest you in?"

Giles nodded. "A map of Bandanarra, if you have such."

"Ah, Bandanarra, is it now? An inhospitable continent, with an abominably hot climate, peopled by the uncivilized and unenlightened. A truly dreadful place." He sighed and got to his feet.

"You've been there?" Giles asked. He would not let the opportunity pass if there was information to be obtained.

Petia raised her eyebrows. "Bandanarra? The continent far to the south? Do you know something you have not told us, Giles?"

"Later," he replied. If he feared Keja and Petia stealing his key, he also feared them appropriating his information before he wanted to reveal it. He turned to the seller. "Have you been there?"

"Ah, no." The huge man heaved another sigh. "In all my life I have gone no farther than half a league from Sanustell. But I have read of the world and of Bandanarra, and twice I have talked with sailors who have sailed along the coast. They tell some awesome tales."

"Don't all sailors?" Giles laughed. "But you do have a map?"

The man rummaged through stacks of maps and finally pulled one from the bottom. He handed it to Giles. Brown with age, it showed crease marks from many ancient foldings.

Giles spread it over a heap of dusty books. The coastline was well mapped and showed numerous ports along the

ocean. But the interior was blank save for a few scattered
—and indecipherable—notations.

He looked up at the bookseller. "There's no detail for the
interior. Surely there is more to Bandanarra than a coastline with some cities scattered along it."

The seller shrugged. "Wastes, deserts, nomadic tribes,
perhaps. You wouldn't want to go there. 'The asshole of the
world,' I have heard it called. With some justice, from all
accounts."

Giles handed the map back to the seller. "It's of no use to
me. I need a more current map, much more detail."

As they walked away, Petia asked, "Do you want me to
steal it for you?"

"It's not a very good map. And I don't like your stealing
needlessly. I've done it, of course, when I was forced to. For
food, bread and cheese, wine sometimes, but I'm never
comfortable with it. I grew sick of the looting and theft
during the War. The key that I won was probably looted."
He laughed. "I guess I have a conscience, after all. It's a
warped one, but it's there just the same."

"What do you mean 'warped'?" Petia asked.

"It doesn't bother me unduly that you and Keja are
thieves. I can't say that I was happy that you tried to burgle
the keys, but otherwise I'm not bothered when you steal.
Don't ask me why. I won't steal, unless I have to or it suits
my purposes, but I'll let you. By the way, I need some paper,
pen and ink. Your skills need sharpening, if last night was
any indication."

"Oh, Giles, I was just a bit drunk. I should never have
attempted it. It was stupid. I'm not even sure why I thought
of doing it."

"It's over. I'm going back to the inn. My shoulder is
bothering me. You stay and enjoy yourself. Don't forget the
paper and pen." He waved and walked off in the direction
of their inn.

Petia licked her lips. This was more like it! She went off
whistling a lilting tune, eyes sharp for possible booths laden
with too many pens and parchment that'd never be missed.

Keja Tchurak found the stall of a swordmaker. He
nodded his greetings and bent to inspect the weapons. They

had a different look to them from the pot-metal blades he wouldn't even deign to steal that were so prevalent in Sanustell. The workmanship of these weapons was nothing less than superb. Picturesque scenes had been engraved on the blades and hilts, turning them into works of art.

"May I examine these?" he asked. Giles still owed him a new sword and dagger after losing his in the cavern of the Flame Sorceress. Of course, he had also mentioned this morning that they were paupers again.

"There is a space in the back where you can swing it without taking anyone's head off," the swordmaker said.

Keja found that the swords had a different heft and feel than what he was accustomed to. He tried several swords but none felt like his old blade. He balanced them across his forefinger and discovered a balance point greatly shifted toward the tip.

He stretched, then shook his arms and hands before picking up one particular sword. Given time, he was certain one would feel comfortable. He set them back in their case. "Beautiful workmanship," he told the swordmaker. "Where did you learn the skill?"

The bearded face turned up to Keja. "Not here, sir. The local swords here are pieces of shit. No balance, no edge, no spine to them. There are several swordmakers on Bericlere who make an adequate weapon. I learned my art on Nerulta, sir. Not a craft, no. An art. My weapons are an extension of my life, the steel quenched in my very own life's blood. These people in Trois Havres don't know a good sword when they see one."

"They don't feel the same as mine."

"You are from . . . ?"

"From Bericlere," Keja replied.

"No, they would not. Bericlere swords generally have soft edges that nick easily, and they balance farther back, so more effort is needed to wield them. Yes, these may seem strange to you, but in a short while you would not regret having purchased one."

Keja shrugged and lifted his palms. "No money."

"I knew that," the old man said. "You will find money if you wish one of my swords. A small warning: do not attempt to steal one. A stolen sword will turn on the thief—always. A sword must be purchased or received as a gift. Never steal a sword, my thief."

"How do you know?"

"I know many things besides the art of making swords. I keep these things to myself, and when I am not busy I ruminate on them. You are young. I think you will not always be a thief. But for now, remember: do not steal one of my swords. Come back with money and we will deal."

Keja grinned.

"I am serious, my friend."

"I know you are. Forgive my nature. I will remember, so you need not worry." Keja nodded to the man and turned from beneath the awning.

He walked directly into a woman. She lost her balance and would have fallen if he had not caught her by the arm. When she was standing again, Keja took off his cap and bowed to her.

An older woman stepped forward. "What do you mean by assaulting my lady?" she demanded in a strident voice.

Aha, a chaperone, Keja thought. He bowed to her. "My deepest pardons, madam. Please forgive me. It was entirely my fault. I turned and should have paid more attention to where I was going. Are you hurt, madam?"

As the chaperone blustered and fumbled, straightening her dress and complaining about rude young men, Keja turned to the young woman and looked into the deepest brown eyes he had ever beheld.

She held her hand over her bosom and red spots appeared on her cheeks. Her breath quickened and the pink tip of her tongue made a slow circuit of her lips. "You startled me, sir. I thank you for catching me before I fell."

"My apologies," Keja said. "Had I not been so clumsy. But . . ." He looked around the marketplace. "I'm sorry, I am unfamiliar with your marketplace, being a traveler from Bericlere. Would you accept tea or some other refreshment? I have always found tea to speed recovery remarkably."

"That won't be necessary," the chaperone cut in. "We have many things to attend to."

"Oh, but we have all afternoon," the young lady said. "Here is my chance to learn about another continent. You always tell me that my geography is bad." Her brown eyes darted to Keja, who smiled even more broadly. He'd be willing to share lessons in geography with this lovely lady any day.

"But we do not know this young man," the older woman protested.

"We know his manners. Did you not tell me that one could perceive the difference between a knave and a gentleman by his manners?"

The chaperone mumbled something to herself, but the younger lady had already turned to Keja. "I am Lady Vaiso. My father owns a small estate at the edge of town. We are rather minor nobles in Trois Havres, I fear, and are not financially well enough off to travel extensively. And you, sir?"

"Thuse Mabein," came the facile lie. "I hail from the seaport of Klepht on the south coast of Bericlere." Keja bowed again. "And now, shall we find that tea?"

The Lady Vaiso took Keja's arm and pointed across the square. They walked away, the chaperone in tow and muttering about impropriety. The swordmaker watched with a smile on his face. Soon, very soon, Keja would return with the price of a fine sword.

Petia found Giles resting on his bed. She set her shawl on the table and flipped open the edges.

Giles sat up and watched. "You weren't wearing a shawl, were you?"

"How observant, sir," she replied. "You sent me on a small quest, but it expanded. By the way, I don't think we can expect Keja this evening. The last I saw of him he was walking arm in arm with an attractive young lady and being followed by a chaperone."

"Ho-ho, chaperones are worse than mythological beasts. And their tongues are sharper." Giles rose and came to the table. "What did you bring?"

Petia spread the shawl. She placed paper, pen and ink in front of Giles, then fetched a plate from a cupboard and arranged stolen fruit, pastries and cheese on it. "Just a little something to dull the appetite," she said. She swirled the shawl around her head and settled it over her shoulders. "Pretty?"

"Very," he said, shaking his head. "I beg your pardon. You have not lost all your skills." He took a bite of cheese, wiped his hand on his trousers and picked up the pen to examine it. "Good quality paper."

"Only the best for you. A small token of my appreciation for not sending me off to indentures. I truly am sorry, Giles. Next time I'll watch my intake. Brandy can get me into trouble."

"Indeed." He opened the bottle of ink and dipped the pen into it. With careful strokes and great concentration, he began to draw. Petia stood behind him, watching over his shoulder.

"Why, it's the map of Bandanarra," she said.

"At least the coastline. This is a skill I learned during the War. No need to buy or steal the map. Just a good memory and a steady hand. That map was not useful, anyway. This will do until we find better."

"Why Bandanarra?"

"That's where the next key is."

"You never said you knew."

"No, I'm not sure that I did know when we first met. I've had some time to think. It goes back to the notation in the holy book I found in the Glanport temple. I just didn't realize what I saw at the time."

"Why didn't you tell us?"

"I wanted to see how well we got along, how well the search for the first key went. I'm cautious by nature."

Petia snorted.

Keja did not show up at the inn for the evening meal. After his second after-dinner pipe, Giles asked of Petia, "Care for a walk along the waterfront? It's time to look for passage."

"Wait until I fetch my knife. It can be rough in waterfront inns."

The harbor was quiet. Light from the dockside buildings reflected in broken shards across the flat water. A few sailors sat on pilings whittling and sharing chanties or along the edge of the wharf fishing. One old sailor was having great success. A tidy string of four fish stared up sightlessly at Giles.

"Any of these ships leaving soon for Bandanarra?" Giles asked after exchanging small talk with the sailor.

"One, I believe, Cap'n." The sailor pointed across to a wharf that jutted into the harbor. "That's the *Raven.* Captain Obidiah. Yer likely to catch him at the Flying Eel." He pointed in the opposite direction down the docks.

"Thank you and good luck with your fishing," Giles said.

"Ain't nuthin' like these and eggs for breakfast. G'night, Cap'n, ma'am."

The Flying Eel was full of boisterous sailors, but Giles sensed that the landlord brooked no rowdiness. Men sat at their ease, as if they knew they could relax there without worrying about a fight.

"Captain Obidiah?" Giles asked. The landlord pointed silently to a corner where an older grizzled man sat with a younger one.

Giles addressed the older man. "Captain Obidiah?"

The gray-haired man grinned and thumbed at the younger man.

"Your pardon, Captain. A natural mistake, I think you'd agree."

"Happens all the time. What can I do for you?"

"We understand that the *Raven* may be leaving soon for Bandanarra. We're looking for passage."

"That's right. Slow passage it will be. Stopping at ports on Bericlere and Nerulta before we proceed on to Bandanarra. Not in a hurry, are you?"

"No. I would guess that there is no swift passage to Bandanarra."

"You'd guess right. Just the two of you?"

"No, one more besides." Giles pulled his pipe out and loaded it.

"Sit and share an ale. I talk better with a wet whistle. I'll bet you do, too. Ma'am, a spot of wine, perhaps?"

Giles and Petia drew up chairs and sat opposite Captain Obidiah. The older man was introduced as Raoul, his mate.

"There is one slight problem, Captain," Giles said. "We don't have passage money. Might we be able to work our passage? We're not able-bodied seamen, but we are all hard workers who learn quickly. We'll give you good measure."

Obidiah rubbed his hand along his chin. "I'm not too keen on that," he said. "Two men I could probably put to work, but, beggin' your pardon, ma'am, I don't know about takin' a lady. That way lies treacherous shoals, if you catch my drift."

Petia bristled. "I've worked ashore in the kitchens of inns. I can peel potatoes, if nothing else. I wouldn't be surprised if I could teach your cook a thing or two. I know rope making, and I'll bet you've got coils that need repairing. I'm not afraid of heights. Send me up in the crow's nest to stand watch. I'm as dependable as most men, and I can hold my own with a weapon."

"Ho, back off. I didn't mean to offend." Obidiah lifted his tankard to Petia.

The conversation turned to Giles. The captain wished to know his background and was impressed with what he learned of Giles' war years. He asked about the third man and listened to Giles and Petia describe Keja.

"What do you think, Raoul?"

"We are short-handed, Captain. We had one leave ship last port, and the cook's stump has been bothering him. I know, I know. He's an old mate of yours for years, but with that wooden leg of his, he could use some help. You don't have much to lose taking them on, Captain. Working passage don't cost you nothing. And if they don't pull their weight, you can drop them off on Bericlere."

Giles chimed in. "No more than fair, Captain. If we don't work as well as you think we should, off we go. Anywhere along your route."

Obidiah nodded, and took a pull from his tankard. He wiped the foam from his mouth, and nodded again, having made up his mind. "The *Raven* sails on the turn of the tide tomorrow evening. Be on her." He held out his hand and shook with both Petia and Giles. It was all the agreement needed.

Keja did not return that evening. At mid-morning he entered their room and dumped a handful of jewelry on the wooden table. "There's our passage," he said, beaming.

"There's our quick way to get shortened a head, you

idiot," Giles snarled, drawing his finger across his throat. "If you had returned last evening, you'd know that Petia and I arranged to work our passage. What are we going to do with this? You won't have time to find a buyer. The young lady, whoever she is, will find her baubles missing, and her father, no doubt a man of considerable power and greater wrath, will have the guard on you in a flash. Perhaps even now they come."

Petia had never heard such exasperation in Giles' voice. Keja's smile had faded, and his abject posture proclaimed his misery.

"I'm sorry, Giles. I was only trying to help. And it was so easy! These gems just begged to be taken!"

"Maybe I can find someone to buy them among the Trans," Petia said.

"We ought to just leave them, dump them down a sewer."

"No!" protested Keja. "I worked *hard* for those!"

Giles frowned. "A burglary is one thing, but to steal from the house where you are a guest is asking for a hanging. They've seen their robber, after all. Get your belongings together. The guard will be here soon, and it must look like you've packed up and gone."

Giles spoke briefly to the thief, then canted his head as the sounds of heavy bootsteps reached his ears. He shoved Keja toward the window. Keja had barely slipped out when a pounding on the door echoed through the room. "City guard," a voice growled.

"Come in," Petia said, hunching over curiously as if her belly troubled her.

"We're looking for Thuse Mabein. We know that he's in your party, although the innkeeper does not recognize that name."

"Nor do we," Giles said. "We traveled from Dimly New with a fellow named Keja Tchurak, the one the innkeeper no doubt mentioned. We are awaiting passage to Bericlere."

"Is this true, lady?" the older of the two guards asked of Petia. He looked at her odd posture and shook his head. She saw the slight drawing forth of the face, the oversized teeth, the round eyes and guessed the guard might be a Trans, also. Petia played on this common bond.

"Yes, would you care to see our papers?" She moved as if

seriously injured and elicited some small sympathy from the older guard.

The two examined the papers, whispering and nodding behind their hands. "And the papers of your companion?"

Giles shrugged. "We are not certain. When we came from the marketplace this morning, his things were gone. He left no note, so we cannot say if he will return or not."

"You don't know where he went?"

"We have no idea," Petia replied. "Why do you seek him?"

The older guard scowled. "A criminal matter." As he talked, he poked about the room, sharp eyes missing nothing. Obviously not satisfied, the guard said, "The sooner you're gone from Sanustell, the better off you will be."

"What?" Giles exclaimed. "Guilt by association?"

"A small warning—your only warning." The guards left.

Petia crept to the door and listened to the receding footsteps. "They're gone," she whispered finally.

"What did you do with the jewelry?" Giles asked.

Petia straightened. She had clutched the pouch with the jewelry to her body; the hunched-over posture had hidden it.

Giles let out a low whistle. Such audacity he had seldom seen. "I told Keja to hide under the wharves. I think you'd better join him while I decoy away the guardsmen."

"But the jewels," she protested. "We can't just let them go to waste."

Giles saw that Keja and Petia were cut from the same cloth. Their devious minds trod the same illicit paths.

"Do as you please with the gems. Just don't get caught. And be there when the *Raven* sails at dusk." Petia's answering smile was more animal than human. Giles shook his head. With companions like these he need never want for diversion.

But just once, how he longed for some peace and quiet!

Petia instantly spotted the city guardsman following her. Although he wasn't in uniform, his stiff manner gave him away.

She ambled casually around the marketplace and amused

herself for a time by losing the guard, then letting him find
her again. All the while, Petia was alert for anyone careless
enough to leave their money pouch outside their clothing.

Lifting a pouch from a roly-poly rug merchant was an
easy matter. Letting him know it was more difficult. But a
second tug on his belt produced the desired result. His yell
could be heard from one end of the market to the other.

"It's him, that one over there," Petia yelled, pointing to
the man who had been following her. "Grab him before he
gets away."

Several other merchants pinned the man to the ground
even as he struggled and proclaimed loudly that he was a
guardsman. No one believed him. A crowd gathered
around, yanked him to his feet and searched him roughly.
Petia seized the opportunity and slipped quietly away. The
small pouch of gold would serve them well. As for the
merchant, if he did not eat so well, his physique might
improve.

A Trans beggar sat along one wall, blind eyes staring up
whitely. Petia deftly tossed one of the rug merchant's
golden coins slightly to the left of the man's container. He
grinned. "Thank you, lady." He scrabbled in the dust, but
his hand knew exactly where the coin had landed.

Petia squatted down in front of him. She watched him
hide the coin in the folds of his tattered robe.

"My pardon," she said. "I gave you the wrong coin. That
was a gold coin, and I meant to give only a copper."

"Oh, no, lady. It was a copper, indeed it was. You see?"
The beggar pulled a copper coin from the same place where
he had spirited Petia's offering.

"So I see," she answered. "I see a blind man who has a
good trade. A blind man who sees as well as I do. Someone
who will give me information. Is that not so?"

The milky eyes did not move, but the lips did. "The War
solved nothing for the likes of us, did it, lady?"

"I seek someone to buy jewelry, a Trans perhaps, no
questions."

Two more gold coins exchanged hands, the directions
were quickly given and Petia left the marketplace. She knew
she'd have to be quick about this. The guard would soon

find the beggar. Even though a Trans, he'd show her no loyalty. The guard would be on her in a shake unless she kept ahead. Petia hastened on, seeing that the guardsman who had been following her had finally convinced the crowd that he had nothing to do with the theft of the rug merchant's pouch. Petia ducked down a side alley, got her bearings and began the search for the one named by the Trans beggar.

She stopped outside a fortuneteller's tent and simply stared. This had to be the place, but it was not as Petia had imagined. The tent flap fluttered in the light, noon-day breeze, and odors both pleasing and oddly intoxicating came to her sensitive nostrils. Almost as if she were drawn forward, she entered the tent.

Dimness caused her cat eyes no trouble. She saw the old woman sitting behind a table, cards spread in front of her. The old woman made a show of moving one card to the far side of the table. Petia knew she had seen her enter; Petia sensed that nothing got past this one unseen.

"I seek Martka," she said in a sibilant whisper. The words boomed forth, frightening her.

"Nothing is as it seems in this place," the old woman responded. "Why does Petia Darya seek Martka of Farplace?"

Petia started to ask how the old woman knew her name, then bit back the question. Such were stock and trade for a fortuneteller. And she also had to know what brought Petia there.

"My business is private," she said. This time the words acted as if smothered in her mouth. Petia preferred this to the former unexpected loudness.

The old woman moved a final card, then sat back, satisfied. "No danger is close at hand," she said. "I will look at the jewelry taken from the fair Lady Vaiso. Her father will ransom it at a good price." The old woman held out her wrinkled, clawlike hand for the merchandise.

Petia silently handed over the pouch containing the jewelry. In the wink of an eye, gold coins dropped onto the table and the jewels had vanished. Petia rubbed her eyes and turned. She stood outside the tent with its odd acoustics and odder odors. Petia swallowed hard when she spun, looked around and glanced back.

The tent with the old woman had vanished totally, as if it had never existed. Only the hard gold of the coins in her hand convinced Petia she had not dreamed it all. As if wings had sprouted on her heels, she hastened back to the inn to tell Giles of her strange encounter.

Chapter Three

The *Raven* coasted along the vast continent of Bericlere, stopping briefly at Neelarna. Giles had to talk Keja out of hunting down the street urchins who had robbed him when the thief had last occasioned by the city. Only loud argument and the captain assigning—at Giles' insistence —Keja to stand watch while in port forestalled a confrontation with the younglings.

The coast of Nerulta came up after Neelarna was long vanished under the horizon, new territory to all three of the companions. As they sailed south, the weather grew warmer, cloudless skies smiled down, and they left green coastal forests behind to look shoreward at golden hills. At ports they found the people darker, the foods and articles for sale unfamiliar.

"The Gentian Coast," sighed Petia. "Here lies real wealth for the plucking." Giles let her and Keja pine over the lost opportunities in the rich area and contented himself with watching the showy blue flowers that grew wild everywhere.

Farther south they left the continent and set course across the Strait of Dunar. At Kasha, the first port of call on Bandanarra, the three said their farewells to the captain.

"We appreciate your letting us work our way," Giles said.

"You gave good work for your passage. If you ever need a steady job at sea, you look for me and the *Raven*."

Giles paid his respects to those who had become friends aboard the *Raven*. He finally threw his bag over his shoulder and led the others down to the wharf.

"I'll have to learn to walk all over again," Petia said. "My knees don't want to work and the ground surges constantly."

"It'll come back," Giles said. "Let's find an inn."

The room they rented for the night was spare of furni-

27

ture, but the thick walls brought a surprising coolness to it. They dumped their belongings on the floor and sat on cotton mats that also served as bedding.

"What now, Giles?"

"The same things we always do. For you, the marketplace for information. Just a general lay of the land, keep your ears open, find out what these people are like. Be careful about picking pockets. It's said that these people could give a master lessons. I'll look through their temples. The holy book I saw in Glanport led us this far. Maybe another here will hand us the key."

Outside the inn Petia and Keja walked toward the marketplace. If they thought that the ports along the Gentian Coast were unusual, they found Kasha even stranger. The people wore long, loose black garments, which looked intolerably hot in the pounding sun. Yet the native population seemed comfortable, while Keja and Petia perspired copiously even when they stayed in the shaded areas.

The bazaar proved little more than a street lined with merchants and shops huddled under tentlike awnings to shelter from the sun. Petia browsed from merchant to merchant, interested in the unique wares displayed. She eventually learned that the heavy-appearing clothing really was cool and was advised that they should purchase similar garments if they intended journeying far from the city and into the desert. Keja, juice running down his chin, motioned for her to sample a fruit sweeter than any he had ever tasted. At a swordmaker's tent, he lingered and cursed his fate that he had not been able to purchase the sword in Sanustell. He regretted passing up such a fine weapon but vowed that Giles would buy him a new sword. Debts ought to be paid, no matter who owed them.

"Look." Petia pointed down the street to the end of the bazaar where cubical cages leaned against the outside wall of a building. "I wonder what those are."

"Probably some sort of animals. Let's go see. You can learn much when you find out what pets people keep."

As they neared the end of the street, they heard piteous cries reverberate from the wall.

"Keja, there are people in those cages!"

He squinted against the glaring desert sun. "You're

right." He turned to a nearby merchant and caught him by a flowing sleeve. "Why are those people in cages?"

The gaunt man turned and looked as if he had never seen the cages before. "Slaves," he said. "To be sold soon."

"How awful," Petia said. She had spent too much of her life as a slave to put this from her mind. The mere thought of her keeper, Lord Ambrose and his evil son Segrinn, made her cringe involuntarily.

They continued from stall to stall, but Petia would lift her head at the sound of each cry. Keja saw abject pain showing in her face. He reached out and lightly touched her arm to reassure her, but the Trans woman pulled away, hissing and clawing at him. She had never adjusted to being a slave.

As they came closer to the end of the market, Petia went to the cages and the people held prisoner within them. Keja spoke and, hearing no response, turned to see Petia gazing toward the cages at the end of the street.

She jerked around and pulled at Keja's sleeve. "There's a Trans there, I know there is. Come on."

"What can you do about it, Petia? It will only upset you." He looked around nervously. In cities where slavery was prevalent, they tended to put thieves onto the auction block rather than imprisoning them. He had no desire to find out if Kasha followed this practice.

Petia glared at him. "I've got to see."

As they neared the cages, an obese man with blubbery lips moved to intercept them. "A slave for my lady?" he asked obsequiously. He bowed, his chins bouncing, then took a quick swipe at his sweaty forehead with a dingy towel.

"How can you keep these people caged up like animals?" Petia pulled free of Keja's restraining hand and shoved her face up close to the merchant's.

The fat man spread his hands. "A business, my lady. For sale, all of them. Perhaps a nice young boy for you? Or an old woman to sweep and cook? The old one will go cheap due to age, but she has many years left in her, perhaps as many as five."

"Come on, Petia. You can't even talk to him about it. He doesn't understand." Keja firmly took her by the elbow to lead her away.

"Wait. There." She pointed. "Look there."

Keja followed her finger to a cage stacked four tiers up. A boy huddled in the back, knees drawn up in a way that reminded Keja of Petia when she sulked. The lean, filthy slave toyed with the end of a rope fastened around his waist. His hair hung in greasy strands making it difficult to make out his age from a distance. "By the gods, he's a Trans!" Keja looked at Petia.

Tears streamed down her face. Her voice choked. "More than that. He's like me, part-cat."

Hearing the word "Trans," the boy scooted to the front of the cage and squatted, hanging on to the vertical bars. "Buy me, lady," he shouted down to Petia.

She confronted the slave dealer. "How much for the Trans boy?" she questioned.

"Auction, my lady. Public auction tomorrow. Come back then. No private sales allowed. Only by bid."

Petia stood before the cage again. She signed to the boy and hoped he understood her dilemma. Then she could not look at him any longer. Turning to Keja, she whispered hoarsely, "Take me away from here."

He saw the devastation in her eyes and said nothing for a long while. Gently he assisted her through the market. He bought a hot, black cup of tiffa, turned tar thick with sugar. He made her sit in a shaded spot along the wall and drink the potent beverage.

"I must get that boy out of there. I'll buy him if I have to." The quiet desperation in her voice told Keja that the boy's rescue had become more significant than anything else. Not the quest for the key, nor even her friendship with Giles and Keja were as important.

When they stood, she cast a despairing look toward the slave cages.

"We'll be back, Petia. I'll help. So will Giles. He won't let the boy stay here."

She walked along in a daze, her mind turning eternally back to the Trans boy. Keja worried about her but kept his eyes open for what Giles had sent them to find. They came to the stall of a dealer in scrolls and maps and for a few moments, Keja turned over the man's maps. He soon realized, however, that he had no idea of what Giles sought.

Keja heaved a sigh of relief when he saw Giles making his way across the crowded street. He waved and attracted Giles' attention, making gestures about the stall. Giles gave a curt nod and walked toward them. His quick eyes scanned the display of maps.

"Your maps are of high quality," Giles said, fingering one. "Good parchment." He frowned and shook his head. "But what use is good material if the map isn't accurate?"

"Sir!" the vendor protested. "These charts are the finest in all Bandanarra!"

"They show the caravan ways, perhaps?" Giles gestured to a stack of maps laying on a table.

"It is so. The desert to the south is the Dus 'i Abat—the desert of skeletons. Many people have died in that desert. You are thinking of journeying there? You cannot find a better map for such a venture."

"I am not certain," Giles said. "I wish to study such a map before I make any decision."

"You lead a caravan? There are spices from the cities on the southern edge of the desert. See? The locations are clearly marked on the fine map. Transporting them north can bring immense wealth."

"Spices hold no appeal," Giles said.

"Aaah." The sigh said much and little. "Perhaps you would share with me?"

Giles studied the map seller. He made a quick gesture silencing Keja's protest about divulging any of their mission. Giles had come to the conclusion this man might aid them. He had the look of knowledge about him—and betrayal, also? That, too, but Giles risked it.

"A gold key. It is said that perhaps it is in the desert." Giles watched for any sign that the man might know what he was talking about. He was surprised at the answer.

First came another long sigh. "The key to the Gate of Paradise. It would not be wise to search for it. No, not wise," the map seller mused. "It is said that it lies hidden in the desert, and many have come over the years seeking it. But there is a religion in Kasha which believes devoutly that it is sacrilege to hunt for the key. It is sacred to their tenets and, it is rumored, they have slain many of the impetuous who sought such a key." He fell silent, and straightened a pile of maps already arranged in near-perfect order.

Giles wondered what had brought about this sudden change from affability to silence. Realizing a hush had settled over all the nearby stalls, Giles turned to look onto the street. Both Keja and Petia had spotted the cause, also.

Two tall, lanky, cadaverous men approached. Cloths wrapping their heads came down almost to their eyebrows. Eyes of burning coals stared out, spreading an aura of contempt, as if the people of the bazaar were mere animals and not worthy of notice. Most of the nearby people had turned their backs rather than look upon the two. The men walked on with stiff, unnatural strides, their heads turning from side to side, disdaining all that came within their sight, human or material.

Giles watched until they disappeared around a corner. "Who were they?" he whispered, struck by the unnatural silence lingering in their wake.

"They are not truly human, or so the people think," the map merchant said, shuddering in spite of the heat. "They are of the desert. A good reason for not venturing there."

"You spoke of a key," Giles reminded him.

"No. No more. If you would learn of the key, ask Pessein, the scribe. He knows more than I. And he is a foolish man, unafraid to talk. It will bring his death one day. Tell him that Ryilla the map seller sent you."

"Thank you," Giles said. "I'll be back for a map." He saw that the man couldn't have cared less and showed only relief at being free of him.

"Giles, I—" began Petia.

"Later," Giles interrupted. "I must find this Pessein. I don't like the looks of those two who went by. They seemed to be searching for . . . something." He couldn't put his uneasiness into words, but he felt the pressure of time mounting.

"But, Giles," said Keja, "Petia's got to—"

"Later. See you later at the inn." Giles had no further time to spend dawdling. He hurried off, leaving Petia and Keja in the bazaar. Giles found the scribe with little effort, and Pessein welcomed Giles, inviting him to share tea. He started a pot of water boiling and gestured to a seat. Giles sat, happy to be out of the sun.

While the tea steeped, the scribe straightened his writing materials and made small talk. Only when he had poured the tea did he settle down to more serious matters. He obviously followed ritual and would not be hurried through it.

"So Ryilla sent you to me. There is something you wish written?"

"No," Giles answered, eager to get to the heart of the matter. "It is information that I seek, information that Ryilla said you may have and that he was afraid to talk about. I wish to learn about the key to the Gate of Paradise."

"You seek it?" At Giles' nod, Pessein pulled at his lower lip. "It is dangerous. Not the story. I care nothing about telling you the story and what I know. But to seek it is foolhardy." He sipped from his bowl.

"My companions and I have journeyed far and have fought to gain what little we have. We know the risks."

"You know nothing," the scribe scoffed. "The key is sacred to the Harifim. Do you know the Harifim?"

Giles shook his head.

"They are a desert tribe, although some live in town. They say that the key keeps the Gate of Paradise locked. They believe that when they die a secret way through the Gate will be revealed to them. They are extremely possessive of the key, although I am not certain that even they know where it is hidden. For a non-Harifim to open the Gate is sacrilege and will deny them their eternal salvation."

"They guard a key whose location is a mystery?" Giles asked.

"The Harifim point off vaguely toward the desert, but they never go beyond that. Why should they aid in their own damnation by helping another through the Gate?"

Giles sipped his tea. "Then, you don't know the location of the key."

Pessein laughed. "Oh, no. I don't want to know. I scribble and I tell stories to pass the time, but I have little desire to know that which might get me killed."

"Do you fear them? Are they so dangerous?"

Pessein looked at Giles for a long moment. "Did you

think it would not be difficult finding your mystical key? The Harifim are a hard desert people. They make enemies easily and friends with difficulty. They do not wish any to be interested in the key. Be careful whom you ask about the key. I am a garrulous fool who seeks only a modest living." He arched one eyebrow. Giles took the hint and dropped several gold pieces onto the table.

Giles stiffened when a shadow bisected a sample of Pessein's craft hung on the wall. "How will we learn if we do not ask questions?" He stood. "Thank you for your hospitality."

Pessein smiled. "Be careful, my friend. And," he added wistfully, "if you do enter the Gate of Paradise, think of me." Pessein sighed and Giles recognized in him a kindred spirit.

As Giles returned to the stall of Ryilla, he kept a sharp eye out for anyone who might be following him. The shadow in Pessein's shop had not been that of a casual passerby. Someone had stood at the window listening —and had been careless for a brief instant.

The map maker looked up with surprise. "I did not expect to see you again."

"I still need a map," Giles said. "The desert."

Petia and Keja entered the stall a few minutes later and found Giles poring over a stack of maps Ryilla had laid out for him. Giles looked up, wondering that they hadn't returned to the inn.

"Have you found what you are looking for?" Keja asked.

"Not yet, but I know it's out there in the desert somewhere." Giles shifted a map, and bent to study the one beneath. Without looking up, he asked, "Has something brought you back? You were going to the inn."

"Giles," blurted Petia, "there's a matter we have to discuss immediately. We have to—"

He silenced her when the map maker came to sit cross-legged in front of him. "You go to look for it, don't you?" Ryilla asked, his dark eyes blazing.

"We go into the desert." Giles moved another map.

"Did not Pessein warn you? There is great danger."

"We don't warn off easily."

"Giles, a word," begged Petia.

"Later." Giles spoke sharply and gestured to the map maker.

"Let me show you, then, the maps with the caravan routes." Ryilla quickly sorted through the stack of maps, pulling out those with routes currently being used. He tossed the others to one side.

Giles immediately moved to a back table, where Ryilla had thrown the older maps. A man perusing various scrolls moved out of his way, and then, nodding to the vendor, left the stall. Some of the maps Giles had already examined, but others he looked at carefully, laying some aside for later scrutiny.

"But," Ryilla insisted, "these are the maps you will need. Is everyone from your country as mad as you? These are *fine* maps!"

Giles looked up and laughed. "We have a saying in our country: 'Madness lies easily upon the back of the hand, and may be seen in the eyes.'"

"I believe that. It must be a good saying because it certainly applies to you." Ryilla shook his head and gestured to Keja and Petia to help themselves to fruit from a nearby bowl. Petia fumed, but Keja took several of the offered fruits.

"Humor him," Keja said. "He will buy. You need not worry over which map it is."

Keja and Ryilla made small talk while Giles continued his search through the old maps. After a half hour, he carried a map to where the three were seated. He laid it down and asked, "Your price?"

Ryilla looked at the map and frowned. "This one?" he asked.

Giles nodded.

"It's over a hundred years old. Routes no longer used. Pictures of mythic creatures along the sides. Useless." Ryilla made it clear by his tone that he thought Giles a little strange. "Look." He pointed, a stubby finger grinding into the parchment. "Cities long abandoned, empty husks of their former glory. Who knows what dwells there now?"

Giles peeled the skin from a fruit and sucked the juice running down his fingers. "How much?" he repeated.

"One darhim to the mad foreigner," Ryilla said with

disgust. "But don't blame me when you get lost. *This* map is far superior to the one you chose." Ryilla held up the one he had originally shown to Giles.

After Giles paid for the map, they left Ryilla shaking his head and muttering about the demented northerner.

"Where to now?" Keja asked. "Petia's got something to say to you."

"The *lirjan* market," Giles said, not hearing more than Keja's question. "We need transportation. That's what we're going to buy, and supplies, and clothing for the desert." Giles finished rolling up the map and strode off, leaving the others to catch up.

The beasts looked awkward and gangling, but Giles knew that for the desert the *lirjan* were infinitely better than horses. Their large, spatulate hooves had evolved to travel easily over the sand. They were only slightly taller than a horse, but were able to survive for long distances in the heat with little water. They could carry two persons for short distances but were much happier with only one.

The market roar deafened Giles as he pushed through the crowd. Vendors shouted that they offered the best beasts. Beneath that were the hoarse, husky grumblings of the animals' voices.

The first broker's smile revealed a mouth full of broken teeth. His obsequious manner made Giles move off to seek another. The manner of the second was better, forthright if not any more honest.

"You must realize, sirs and lady, that I will receive shaharm when you buy. A fee from each side of the transaction, if you will. But I will try to recommend animals who are healthy and strong and can be obtained for a reasonable price. Gashmeen is renown for his services, his fine animals provided to discerning travelers such as yourselves." Giles saw that this amounted to little more than bragging, but Gashmeen appeared to do a thriving business. This, if nothing else, recommended him.

"We ask no more," Giles said, handing over the gold equivalent of the five darhim required.

It was an exhausting, time-consuming task. Long before it was finished, Giles knew that Gashmeen had earned his money. The broker examined the animals from a distance at first, looking at their conformation and their stance. When he had selected some to examine more closely, he found out the price being asked. If it was within the range that Giles had suggested, he continued with his examination. Teeth, nostrils, legs, coat, all were observed carefully. He would even lift their tails and study the anus.

"I'm glad he's not examining me," Keja said.

Evening was upon them before the beasts were selected and the bargaining done. For two additional darhim, the broker arranged for care of the animals until the trio was ready to leave.

"It's too late now," Giles said, acknowledging the evening dusk. "But tomorrow we must shop for clothing and supplies."

"Thank the gods," Keja exclaimed. "Me for a flagon. It's not the same fine ale as at home, but it'll do. Moistens the throat well enough."

"A bowl of fruit for me," Petia said, resigned to speaking with Giles later about the slave boy. "I've never tasted so many different fruits with such delicate flavors."

As they entered the inn, Giles saw a shadow again on the wall. He spun, then shouted, "Down!" His quick reflexes saved Keja from a knife in the back. A heavy-bladed hunting knife cartwheeled through the air and loudly *thunked!* into the wooden door.

"We're being warned off," Petia said, pointing to the scrap of paper impaled by the knife.

Giles took the paper and read the inscribed message, then handed it to Keja. "The scribe warned me that the Harifim don't like people asking about the key. We'll have to be more careful."

During the evening a man, old and grizzled, entered the inn. His hunched back looked bent under the woes of the world. He rubbed his hands as if they were cold, although the sun had only set an hour before. The innkeeper intercepted him as he walked across the common room and started to turn him out. Petia sat lost in her own thoughts while Giles and Keja discussed their trip into the desert. She saw the old man's plight and felt sorry for him. Rising from the table, she motioned to the landlord.

Taking the old one by the arm, she invited him to have a cup of mint tea laced with beldon leaves. The man nodded eagerly. "Tea in exchange for a story. I give you a story."

"We are newly arrived in Kasha," Petia told him. "Perhaps you would tell a story about your city or the desert." She tried to forget the slave pens and the Trans boy. Somehow, Petia thought by showing kindness to the old man she might take her mind far away.

His grin was toothless, but endearing. His ragged clothing seemed clean, and quick eyes darted around the table, taking in the map Giles pored over. The man took a sip of tea and sighed. Wiping his mouth with the back of his hand, he looked around the table. "What stories would you have me tell?" he asked.

Giles put away the map, drew a coin from his pouch and laid it on the table. The old man's eyes gleamed, and he smiled. "A tale of the desert, perhaps," Giles said. "A tale concerning a key many centuries old—a key sacred to the Harifim."

A frown crossed the leathery face, adding creases to the creases. "Dangerous. It is dangerous to talk about the key. You speak of the Harifim, a fierce, unforgiving people. It is good to avoid them. Even those who have come to live in the city; they retain their ways. A savage people, warlike, very dangerous." The old man shook his head. "It would be good to avoid them," he repeated.

Giles took up his pipe and loaded it with tobacco. The man's eyes watched him, birdlike. His eyes pleaded that he be allowed to tell a different story.

Giles lighted his pipe and said between puffs, "The Harifim believe the key is an important part of their religion. Do they have a temple in the city?"

The old man looked down at the table and then sipped from his mug. He played the game nearly as well as Giles.

"It is said that the key keeps the Gate of Paradise locked. Only the Harifim find a secret entrance when they die. They believe that the key is in the safekeeping of the Skeleton Lord, who lives in an abandoned city in the desert."

"And where is this city?" asked Keja.

"I do not know, but you must have seen the Lord's creatures in the city. They are so lean that they look like skeletons. Their eyes are sunk so deep into the sockets that one can never see them, can never read anything but death in them. People are afraid of them. Merchants deal with them quickly and with great courtesy so that they may be rid of them. The Harifim fear them, also, if they are afraid of anyone."

Giles puffed thoughtfully. "Tell me of the skeleton men. Where do they come from?"

"The desert." The old man's hands encompassed the width and breadth of the desert outside the city. "They could be from anywhere. There are many lost cities out there. Dead for hundreds of years. The Skeleton Lord lives in one such, or so it is said. The desert is their world." He rubbed his forefinger through some spilled tea and made circles on the table.

He stood up. "That is all I know. Please do not say that I have told you these things. Leave the desert alone. I speak too much for a cup of tepid tea." The old man bowed and left.

"What do you make of that?" asked Keja.

"Another warning sent us," said Giles, puffing thoughtfully on his pipe. "Less emphatic than the knife, but still a warning."

"'A warning? Sent by whom?" asked Petia, pulled out of her worry over the boy.

"That is something we'll find out," Giles said, "soon."

Chapter Four

"They can't get away with that!" Keja said hotly. "We can't let them—whoever 'they' are—come in here any time they want and rummage through our belongings."

"Listen to who's talking. The old master thief himself. Now you know what it's like to be robbed." Giles lounged back and studied the small, slightly disordered room. He suspected those responsible for stealing what little they had of value to be the Harifim. But to prove it? Impossible. "All we're out are a few coins—and the map."

"Why would they steal it?" asked Petia. "They know their way through the desert."

"It's to keep us from finding the key," said Keja, still angered by the intrusion into their rooms. "I, for one, am not going to let them get away with it. We'll steal their damned key and spit in their eyes doing it! Wait and see!"

"It's off to the marketplace," Giles said. "I didn't study that map enough to be able to duplicate it." He frowned and scratched his head.

"What is it, Giles?" Keja paced furiously and only occasionally slowed. "Something occur to you?"

"Just trying to think of those who knew I had the map." The old man Petia had offered the tea to had known, but Giles decided he was only a minion of another who already knew.

He left to question Ryilla about the stolen map.

On the way, he passed a secondhand shop, saw the clutter inside and on an impulse entered to look over the old carpets, leather tent flaps, brass utensils, broken swords and other unidentifiable items littering the floor. Within a few minutes he had found a pile of old maps. One showed caravan routes across the desert.

Giles studied it carefully. Drawings of beasts from some

40

ancient desert mythology adorned the map along its edges.
The portraits appealed to his sense of humor. He compared
the map with his memory of the maps examined the
previous day. These routes differed from the ones on
Ryilla's more recent maps.

He paid a shambling old woman who appeared from
behind a curtain at the back of the room. She examined him
with rheumy eyes and bit the coin he handed her. "Thank
you, mother," he said as she relinquished her hold on
the map. Giles didn't see her toothless grin as he left the
shop.

He continued up the street, intent on talking to Ryilla
once more. Before he reached the marketplace he tucked his
recent purchase inside his tunic. The vendor did not need
to know that he had replaced the map with one better suited
for his purposes.

When Giles reached the small shop, the dealer was all
smiles. "Ah, good sir. Back to buy another map?"

"Back to find out who you told about selling me the map
yesterday." Giles' face was stern. He dropped a canvas flap
over the door and put out the small brass pot indicating
that the shop was closed. He had reached the end of his
patience with the grinning Ryilla.

"Surely, there is a mistake," the map seller said, his grin
hollow now. His dark eyes darted about, seeking an escape
route. Giles was no man to argue with. "Why would I wish
to do such a thing? Not for the sake of selling you another
map for a darhim or two."

"Then, you know that it was stolen." Giles pinned the
man against a wall like a bug on a pin.

Color drained from the already gray face. "I know
nothing of the sort. I would not have someone steal it back
to sell again."

"I don't think you would," Giles replied. "But I think
you would tell the Harifim that a stranger was asking too
many questions. I wonder if you are not of the Harifim
yourself."

"And if I were?" Ryilla looked toward a torn corner of
the tent. Giles turned to see eyes staring back at him. "I
would warn you away from the desert. The key is sacred to
my people. The faithful are lent the key when they die so

that they may enter Paradise. You put yourself in grave
danger if you go to steal it!" Perspiration beaded the map
seller's forehead. "You would do well to turn around and
sail back to your home."

"Not likely," Giles replied. "One key would not do
you or your friends a bit of good. It takes five to open the
Gate."

Ryilla's mouth hardened into a line and his eyes blazed.
"Heresy! There is only one key."

"There are five locks, each requiring a separate key. I
know. I've seen the Gate."

"Liar!" Ryilla roared. "You cannot have seen it. Only the
Harifim are allowed. Our key alone will open the Gate."

"I don't think you even know where this key is, this single
key you speak of," Giles said softly.

Ryilla waved his hand and men poured into the tent.
Giles had wondered how long it would be before those he
had seen spying entered. If all went well, he might learn
something of value now.

"This man is blaspheming against our faith," Ryilla said
angrily, grinding his teeth. "Take him to the temple and
lock him in a cell. You need not be careful of how you treat
him."

Giles did not see the haft of the dagger flash toward the
back of his head. Nor did he feel the pain from the blow. He
was unconscious before the message reached his brain.

Keja had vanished, but Petia paid no heed. She stared up
at the young boy in the wooden cage. Hanging onto the
crude bars, he knelt at the front, looking down imploringly
at her.

His clothes hung in tatters, and Petia saw ribs sticking out
of his scrawny chest. She wondered how he had gotten into
this situation. Where were his parents? Dead? Brothers and
sisters? Perhaps he had none. She swallowed hard. Was she
in any better condition? Her family had died during the
Trans War, and the threat of Segrinn still plagued her. How
could she forget his brutalities, the way he hunted her down
even now, the punishments in store for her if he found
her?

The slave dealer walked toward Petia, rubbing his hands

unctuously. "My lady is interested in the boy, yes?"

For a brief moment Petia thought to rip out his throat with her claws, but she quieted her rampaging emotions. "Yes," she answered. "He is a Trans, like myself."

"The auction will begin in a half hour. There are slaves who will sell for much more money than he. I don't expect that he will come to the block until late afternoon."

Petia stared into the slave dealer's eyes. He averted his gaze. "That's all right," she said. "I have a great deal of patience and nothing else to do."

"As my lady wishes." The man turned and waddled off, glad to be away from the crazy Trans.

Petia settled gracefully to the ground, stirring the dust beneath her. She would have the boy. Nothing would deter her from purchasing him—or stealing him, if that proved necessary. Giles would be furious, and it might mean the end of her part in their quest, but she did not care. Giles had ignored her the day before to the point she had ceased trying to mention it. He seemed too wrapped up in the intrigue surrounding the map and its theft to bother with freeing a poor Trans boy.

Patiently she watched cages being unlocked and humans pulled onto the raised stage and displayed like livestock. Many seemed relieved when they were purchased; their waiting was over. No matter the situation they might be entering, at least it would be stable and a known quantity.

The sun beat down with increasing ferocity as Petia waited, signing to the boy to be patient. She watched as nubile young girls, men shrunken with age, haggard old women, and other young boys were led to the block. She heard the eager shouts of various bidders, "Five darhim, ten darhim, twenty darhim." And she looked elsewhere when the sale consummated so that she wouldn't see how new owners treated their new slaves.

After long hours of waiting, the Trans boy's cage was opened. The slave master's assistant gestured for him to come down from the fourth tier. The boy scrambled down, using his arms while his legs dangled free. When he reached the bottom, Petia saw that he walked with one leg twisted awkwardly. He limped to the block.

"A healthy Trans boy," the slave master shouted. "He

limps only because he has been crowded into the cage. The kinks will work themselves out. His legs are as sound as my own."

The boy shook his head negatively from his crouched position.

"What am I bid for this fine boy, only eleven years of age? Unwanted by his parents but strong and with many good years of service in him."

Petia's voice rang clearly over the heads of the crowd in front of her. "Fifty darhim." The crowd hushed, then gabbling broke out over so high a starting bid. It was traditional to start with five or less darhim.

"Five darhim has been bid," the slave master shouted. "The lady begins the bidding at five darhim."

"No, O greasy one. Fifty darhim." Petia's gaze did not waver as the crowd turned to examine her. She heard people near her exclaiming: "She must really want the boy"; "It's too bad he is a cripple"; "No one will bid that high for him. She could have had him cheaper."

The slave master wiped his forehead. "Fifty darhim," he shouted, "for this excellent boy. He is Trans, part-cat. Do I hear fifty-five? Fifty-five darhim, going once."

Petia's voice rose once again. "A trick one might expect from such as you, fat-as-a-sow. My bid is fifty darhim, not fifty-five. Shall we now say 'fifty darhim, going twice?'"

The crowd laughed at the slave master. He shouted, "Fifty darhim, three times." The crowd continued to chuckle at his discomfiture. "Sold for fifty darhim. Take the accursed cripple." He pushed the boy off the stage. The boy turned and bowed to the slave master, then raised his arms and did a dance step on perfectly straight legs. When he had finished, he bowed to the slave master again, then turned to greet Petia.

Petia touched her empty pouch—the intruders had stolen her money—but still she smiled as she stepped forward, pushing through the crowd. Her nimble fingers worked and purses opened at her passing. By the time she reached the slave master, she had more than the fifty darhim required —and it had all been supplied by the very people she hated most.

"Stand up, boy," she said when he tried to pay her

obeisance. "Such behavior offends me."

"Mistress, let me kiss your feet. I would do anything for you."

"If that is so, then stand up and don't embarrass me. Why did you pretend to be a cripple?"

The boy rose from the dust and looked up into her face. "I had hoped that you would purchase me. I wanted to go cheaply so that you would not be angry. I was trying to save you some money."

"You are a rascal. What is your name?"

"Anji, my lady."

"All right, Anji. First we see about something to eat, then some decent clothing for you."

"But these clothes will be all right. Mistress has paid good money for me. I am content to be out of the cage. I will work hard for you, you will see. And I eat little."

"You will eat what I tell you. You're scrawny. Your ribs stick out. Now be quiet for a moment while I think where to take you for food."

The boy's eyes widened when he saw that Petia meant to take him to a café. "I have never eaten in one of those, Mistress. I would not know what to do."

"Then, it is time for you to begin learning, is it not?" She took his hand and pulled him along behind her.

Once seated in a café, Petia ordered plain food and, when it came, leaned back in her chair. She enjoyed the sight of the near-starving boy as he wolfed down the food. After a few minutes, she made him slow down and showed him how to use the table implements: the spoon for the soups and stews, the fork for vegetables and meat, and the knife for cutting.

Sensing the boy's awkwardness, she encouraged him. "You'll do fine with practice."

At last Anji sat back, groaning. His stomach hurt from so much food after existing on bare rations for such a long time. He put his hands on his belly and said, "It hurts."

"You've gone hungry for a long time, then?" Petia asked.

"Since I was sold to the slave master."

"When was that?"

"A long time ago, Mistress. I was sold once before, but I didn't work hard enough, and my owner sold me back to the slave master. But I will work hard for you, Mistress. I will do whatever you command."

"I didn't buy you to be my slave," Petia said. "I bought you to set free. After I get you some decent clothing, you can go wherever you want. Do you understand? You are free."

The boy's eyes opened wide. He shook his head. "Do you mean that I am to go away. Where will I go? I want to stay with you, Mistress."

"I'm not sure that you can do that, Anji. I have obligations to other people. I'm not certain that they would allow you to accompany us. It would be best if you went your own way." Petia's heart dropped as she said the words; she found the boy appealing. He was a Trans, part-cat as she was, and alone in the world. She knew the feeling.

"Where are your parents?" she asked.

Anji turned sullen. "I don't know. I don't care, either. They sold me to the slave master. They didn't want me."

Petia closed her eyes. So Anji had been rejected by his parents, too. Her own father was long dead, but it was her mother who had indentured her to Lord Ambrose. Clearing her mind of the painful memories, she took the boy by the hand and went in search of a clothing shop.

A much more presentable Anji followed Petia into the room at the inn. She didn't know which of them was the more nervous. Anji had never been allowed inside an inn before, and she was unsure of Giles' reaction to the foundling. She saw no sign of Giles but found Keja staring out the window. He whirled as she and Anji entered.

"Where have you been?" he asked. A worried look creased his brow.

"I'd like you to meet Anji." The boy peered up at Keja, although there wasn't that much difference in their heights.

"The slave boy," Keja said, finally recognizing the youth. "Hello, Anji. You haven't seen Giles, have you?" Keja asked, returning his gaze to Petia.

"No. Why? You look worried."

"He said he'd be back early this afternoon. He hasn't returned or sent any message. You didn't see him in the market?" Keja persisted.

"I don't think there's anything to worry about. Giles knows his way about, and he looked as if he had much to do when he left this morning. He'll show up."

"I'm going out to look for him. Don't you go wandering off." He almost ran out of the room.

Petia barely had time to relax over a cup of scented tea when Keja returned, downcast. "Did you speak to the map seller?" she asked.

"He admitted that Giles had been there and had looked at some more maps. Giles asked about temples, and the map seller—Ryilla, I think his name is—said that he directed him to several around Kasha."

"Ryilla," Anji said. "That is the map seller's name. A Harifim. Be careful of him."

"How do you know that?" Petia asked.

"My previous owner was of the Harifim. Bad people, he beat me. Ryilla is Harifim, also."

Keja sighed. "And the Harifim have warned us not to search for the key. Not in so many words, but a knife in the back can say more than words alone."

"And Giles has gone to the Harifim temple to see what he can uncover," Petia concluded.

"They are fanatics," Anji said. "They would capture your friend, about whom you worry, and hold him at the temple if they thought he tried to get information about their cult. This Ryilla is the guilty one. He gave your friend over to the Harifim. He is one of them!"

"We'd better go see if Giles is in trouble," Keja said. "If he is, we can break into the place and get him away."

"You do not know the Harifim, sir," Anji said. "They are savage. They have guards in their temple. It would be best to wait until nightfall. At vespers their ceremony will be at a point where most of them will be in a trance from a drug they use. You will have a much better chance of getting in."

The waiting was unbearable. Keja and Petia hoped to see Giles walk in the door at any moment, but as the dinner hour passed and the sun sank into the hot desert sands and promised a modicum of coolness, Keja became more nervous. Finally he reached into his pack and took out a rope. He wound it carefully around his waist, then flung on his cloak. Petia took her cloak from the hook by the door.

"You stay in the room, Anji, until we get back. Do not go anywhere, do you understand?"

"Yes, Mistress." The boy's eyes gleamed with excitement, but he sat meekly with his hands folded in his lap. "You do not know where the temple is," he said calmly.

Petia muttered in exasperation. "No, but you'll tell us how to reach it, and then you will stay *here,*" she insisted.

Using Anji's somewhat muddled directions, they found the Harifim temple, which stood stark against the low desert moon, casting elongated shadows across the square. The building was plain, only two stories high, with a flat roof. There was no dome or tower or other rooftop ornamentation. Neither had ever seen a temple like it.

"Catch the lip of the roof with your hook," Petia whispered. "You stand watch while I take a look up there."

Keja knew better than to argue and unwound the rope from his waist. He attached a triple hook to one end and tied the knot carefully. It caught the ledge on the first try; he tested it with his weight before stepping back.

Petia flexed her fingers, grabbed the rope and paused, concentrating. Mentally she shifted herself to a more feline orientation, becoming more agile, quicker, her body turning sleeker. She pulled the rope taut and scurried catlike up the wall to the roof. Keja watched in open admiration.

She paused briefly at the edge of the roof, and Keja saw her crouch and peer into the darkness. The Trans turned and signaled that she would leave the hook and rope in place.

Her first glance suggested that there would be no way into the temple from the flat roof, but previous experiences at thievery cautioned her that first impressions were not always true. She circled and, finding nothing, crossed the roof from side to side, studying and feeling its surface with preternaturally sensitive fingers. At the halfway point, she felt the roof give slightly. Kneeling, she discovered a trap door, flush with the roof. Her claws slid under the edge of the door; she lifted carefully.

A ladder led downward into the Harifim stronghold. She went down catlike, head and hands first, and came out in a narrow passage. Lifting her head, she tried to identify the strange scent permeating the air. Spicy and pungent, it was unlike anything she had smelled before. The first sniff cleared her head, as if she had been suffering from a cold. The second made her giddy.

The sound of drums, beating softly but with rhythmic intensity, came from beyond the wall. Then she felt that peculiar rhythmic vibration of people dancing.

Petia moved cautiously down the bare-walled passage until she came to an open archway. Keeping her head low, she peered around the corner into the room. Several men stood watching, intent on the scene before them.

There were no women in the room. Except for a few guards, all the men were involved in the dance. Some had reached a trance stage and fallen to the floor. It was evidently the duty of the nonparticipants to drag the entranced ones out of the way of the dancers. The men still on their feet went through the peculiar dance steps with their eyes closed. They held their arms out to the side, almost as if they were wings, and dipped and glided for a few beats of the drum, a parody of some great bird of prey. Then, in a great flurry, they whirled five or six times. The motion was repeated again and again.

Petia did not worry about the trance dancers. Only the watchers worried her. Backing away from the archway, she crept down the passageway. At each doorway she peered in cautiously but found only empty rooms. Eventually she came to a set of stairs leading downward.

She descended into the main body of the temple. An altar stood near one end of the room, and intricately woven prayer mats covered the floor. No guards, no supplicants, no one. She saw only two doorways. One led from the front of the temple and was the main entrance from the street. The other she stood in.

Petia started to leave, then stopped, a strangeness to the room making her uneasy. She wrinkled her nose. It was not quite a musty smell, not the odor of a building dried and desiccated by the sun-beaten desert. A humid, almost cool feeling to this room reached out and touched her face, her hands. Repressing a shiver, she walked quietly toward the altar.

A simple desert cloth adorned it. Behind the altar table a

tapestry bright with geometric patterns of talismanic significance stretched across one wall. After studying the eye-confusing pattern, she decided it certainly did not picture a scene on this world. She felt the heavy desert cloth and, on impulse, flicked back one edge.

Behind it a narrow passage meandered off to end in a hole in the floor. Narrow treads led down into a subterranean passage. Thanking the gods for feline vision, she descended. Moist earthen walls immediately answered the question of the strangely humid smell.

Petia closed her eyes and listened intently. She heard disturbed breathing and ventured a quiet call. "Giles?"

A groan sounded in response. She followed the faint cries of pain and found a rough door, barred on the outside. She called again, but no answer came, not even a moan.

She lifted the bar, set it carefully along the wall and opened the cell door.

Giles Grimsmate lay in a crumpled heap in one corner of the room. She went to him, her heart in her throat. He had been beaten until almost unrecognizable. His breath rattled in his throat.

Petia put her hands on his forehead. "Giles, can you move?"

Even with her superior night vision, she could barely see in the dark cell. She tried to rouse Giles but could get nothing more from him than the intake of a short breath, which set him coughing. She could not even tell if he was conscious.

"Giles, wake up." No response.

Petia grimaced. She needed help, and Keja was outside. She would have to go all the way up to the roof to signal him, and the gods only knew how they would get Giles out.

Not liking the idea of traversing the Harifim temple but seeing no way around it, Petia made her way quickly and silently to the roof. In a few minutes, she had signaled Keja and, when he joined her, explained the situation.

"We only waste time," he told her. "The sooner we get back to the basement and rescue Giles, the sooner we can be gone from this accursed temple." They retraced Petia's earlier route past the guards and dancers, into the nave and the passage and down to the cell.

Gathering the older man, Keja lifted him to his shoulders. "If we get him out of here without arousing those acolytes, it will be a miracle," he said. "Giles is heavier than I expected. Lead on."

Keja staggered under Giles' weight, but they gained the temple's main floor without incident. Keja leaned against the wall to catch his breath without putting Giles down.

"The next part is going to be tricky," Petia whispered. "Try not to breathe too loudly. There are four guards watching the dancing. If we get past them, we have a chance of getting out of here. If we can't . . ." She left the sentence unfinished.

The narrow, steep steps forced Keja to struggle constantly for balance. The inert Giles was a dead weight, arms dangling and sometimes swinging from the motion. Keja reached the top of the stairs and concentrated on breathing quietly, almost an impossibility.

Petia motioned for Keja not to rest—too much danger. She pointed to the room where fewer feet could be heard dancing. More of the men had succumbed to the drugs and spin dancing.

Heaving a deep breath, Keja moved to the foot of the ladder leading to the roof. He raised his right foot and placed it on the first rung. Against his shoulder he felt Giles take a deep breath. When the unconscious man let out the air, a deep moan echoed down the passageway.

Keja looked apprehensively at Petia, who motioned him on up the ladder. She heard a short exclamation in the desert language, followed all too quickly by the sound of feet rushing toward them. Four acolytes rounded the corner of the archway.

Petia drew her sword and shouted over her shoulder at Keja. "Hurry. I'll hold them off."

She crouched, sword at the defensive. The men advanced, although they were unarmed. They obviously intended to bowl her over with their sheer numbers, even though she might kill or injure one or two.

They were still several feet away from her when a yell echoed from the temple room below. "Hadrani! Arifa! Hadrani!"

Several voices came from below. Petia couldn't understand the language, but the emotion was clearly one of panic. "Hadrani!" the voices repeated. The men confronting Petia exchanged frowns. One shook his head and took another step toward her. A second man stopped, sniffing the air. "Hadrani," he growled, and sniffed again. The others sniffed, then rushed at Petia. To her amazement, they went right past her and disappeared down the stairway to the main temple room.

"Up the ladder quickly," Keja shouted. "Pull it up behind you."

Atop the temple roof, they staggered to the edge. "You first," Keja said. "Then I'll lower Giles."

In only moments, Keja reached the ground and shouldered Giles again. As they melted into the shadows playing along the street opposite the temple, Anji joined them.

"Did I do good?" he asked.

Petia grabbed the boy's arm. "What are you doing here? I told you to stay in the room."

The boy's eyes sparkled as the small band entered the moon-soaked square. "Hadrani. Hadrani," he said in a deep voice not his own. "That is 'flee!' in the language of the desert."

"You? Downstairs in the temple?"

Anji nodded. "I set a small fire with paper. Lots of smoke. Lots of voices, too. I did three or four men from different corners. I followed you. It is not good to go against the Harifim without someone at your back."

Petia tried to be angry with the boy and failed. "We'll talk about this later. Keja, hurry. They'll be after us for certain now. We'd better tend Giles, then gather our belongings and leave the inn."

"Where will we hide at this time of night? We don't know the city."

"Anji does. We'll find a place."

They entered the inn through the kitchen and hurried up the back stairs to their room. They stripped Giles and, with a clean cloth dipped in wine, Petia tended the bloody abrasions on his body. He gained consciousness briefly, but his eyes never focused and he closed them again.

"Anji, think of somewhere we can hide." Petia wiped the wine-soaked cloth across a cut in Giles' forehead.

"Where do you go next?" the boy asked. "You are obviously travelers from another country."

"We were going into the desert. We've bought supplies and several *lirjan.*"

"Where are the *lirjan*?" Anji asked.

When he heard Petia's answer, he said, "So. Hide in the caravanserai among the *lirjan*. They might not find us there. The Harifim come from the desert, where they prey on caravans. They are not at all welcome among other travelers."

Petia found that Giles had no broken bones, but he sucked in his breath noisily when she touched his ribs. She bound them tightly, hoping that none was cracked. A sip of wine forced into his mouth seemed to revive him a bit. He started to talk, but Petia shushed him.

"We've got to leave right now, Giles. Can you walk?"

"Dunno," he mumbled. With Keja on one side and Petia on the other, he managed to get to his feet. They walked him across the room and back.

"He'll make it if he can lean on both of us and we go slowly," Keja said. "What about our belongings?"

"I carry them," Anji spoke up. He gathered the packs together and slung them over his skinny shoulder.

Keja raised his eyebrows at the boy's strength but shook his head ever so slightly at Petia, warning her to let Anji have his own way. The boy had a great deal of pride and had helped them immensely tonight.

They left the inn quietly and let Anji lead them. Through deserted back streets they reached the caravanserai. The tent guard grumbled at the lateness, but Keja slipped him a coin to quiet him.

They found a place in the middle of the gathering and lowered Giles to the ground, placing a pack beneath his head. His eyes opened briefly. "Thank you, friends," he whispered. "The map." He lifted his hand and pointed at the back of his trousers.

"But it was taken," Keja said, frowning. When Giles motioned again, Keja rolled him over and groped inside. When his hand came out, the folded map was between his fingers. Keja frowned even more when he saw the map. "Not the same one," he said.

"Giles found a better one," Petia said with confidence.

Keja tucked the map out of sight in his own tunic, then asked, "Now, what do we do with the boy?"

Anji knelt in front of Petia, his eyes imploring her. She looked from Anji to Keja and back again. "If we don't take him with us, he's dead. The Harifim will see to it."

"He'll only be in the way if he comes with us. Giles will be furious."

"He wasn't in our way earlier this evening, Keja. Either he goes with us, or I don't go. And don't go putting words in Giles' mouth." She glared at Keja.

Keja muttered for a moment, then subsided, shaking his head. "All right, but he's your responsibility. And you can explain it to Giles."

"Yes, he is and I will." Petia gestured to a space on the ground. "We'll sleep there." She lay down and threw her cloak over the boy and herself. They listened briefly to the night noises of the *lirjan* before they slept. Petia's sleep was troubled by visions of drug-crazed Harifim pouncing on her from the darkness.

Chapter Five

"Caravaners for Kuilla, rise up, rise up! Kuilla only. Line up your *lirjan* against the south wall." The cry rang through the caravanserai. *Lirjan* grunted as drivers prodded them to their feet.

Petia blinked open her eyes and for a panicked instant thought she'd gone blind. The blackness of the sky above was relieved by only one or two twinkling stars. She stretched and got circulation flowing through tired veins, then roused Anji and kicked Keja to get him awake. "Up, sleepy head, the day's half gone," she said with feigned exuberance.

She knelt by Giles. "How are you feeling? The caravan for Kuilla is preparing to leave."

"Kuilla? Help me up, will you?"

Petia assisted him. Giles winced at the pain in his ribs. "You and Keja go take care of getting us a spot in the caravan line."

Giles struggled to get their packs buckled up while the others took care of their duties. He rubbed his side and decided the injury wasn't too bad. He cursed himself for being so stupid and thinking he could learn of the key by allowing himself to be kidnapped by the Harifim. If it hadn't been for his friends, he would have died in the Harifim prison. And to make matters even worse, he had gained no new knowledge for the effort.

He swung the pack up and settled it into a comfortable spot on his back when a boy ran up to him. "Master Giles, Petia says that the *lirjan* are in line. We can pack them there."

"Thank you, boy. This for your trouble." He spun a coin into the air.

The boy caught it deftly and tossed it back. "I cannot take

it, Master Giles. Come, this way. I show you." He pulled at Giles' sleeve.

"Where did you get this little charmer to help you?" Giles asked as he joined the others by their animals.

"I bought him yesterday at the slave market. He is mine," Petia replied.

"What?" Giles exploded.

"I offered him his freedom, but he wants to stay with me. I can't turn him down. He goes with us."

"We can't take a child with us," Giles said. "We don't have any idea what's ahead—except for more trouble. Who's going to be responsible for him? We don't have enough supplies. He'll be in the way. He could get sick. He doesn't have a *lirjan* to ride." Giles paused for breath and finally added, "And you shouldn't have bought him. Never give so much as a fart to those who deal in human flesh and misery."

Petia let him run through the litany of reasons the boy shouldn't accompany them. When he ran out of breath, she said quietly, "Anji goes with me. Or I don't go."

"No, Petia. We cannot afford someone who will be in the way."

"He wasn't in the way last night when Keja and I pulled you out of the Harifim temple. If it hadn't been for him, all three of us would be in that cell right now, instead of getting ready to leave Kasha." Petia turned and looked back toward the city. "He stays with me," she said again, returning her unblinking gaze to Giles.

"Hummph! On your head, then!" Giles grumbled before he busied himself with unneeded repacking.

The half dark of false dawn still clung tenaciously to the desert when the last *lirjan* cleared the city gates. For a time the caravan followed a well-beaten track that led past a series of wells outside Kasha's walls. Gradually the track dwindled to a single rut stretching into the desert.

"I had hoped that we would group up and be shielded from prying eyes," Giles said. "The Harifim know what we are seeking. They'll be after us, I fear. Keep a careful watch."

They soon fell into the rolling, awkward gait of the *lirjan,* although Giles winced with pain at every misstep the animal made. Seeing that the caravan made good time and that the Harifim would be unable to approach without being sighted, Giles reached for the map.

"Gone!" he cried. "They got the map!"

Keja put his heels to his animal's flanks and trotted up beside Giles. "Here. Took it to make sure it wasn't lost. Didn't want you bleeding on it."

Giles heaved a sigh of relief. He'd been through too much to get this map to have it lost due to his own miscalculations. He didn't bother with the ancient caravan routes; he examined the map's illuminated borders. Around the perimeter cavorted mythical beasts of fantastic proportion and viciousness. There weren't creatures anywhere that looked like those represented in the drawings. There couldn't be.

Giles squinted into the morning sun at the long string of *lirjan* stretching out into the desert. He turned on his mount to look back at a line nearly equal in length before scanning the desert on both sides for any hint that the Harifim pursued them. Heaving another sigh of relief when he found no trace of the fanatical cultists, Giles decided he might be overestimating the Harifim's devotion to protecting their key to the Gate of Paradise.

Returning his attention to the beasts inked onto the map, he wondered how a scribe would dream up such creatures. In the upper right-hand corner an upright creature glowered, standing on two ponderous legs and covered with tiny scales. The slim torso widened to a mighty chest and shoulders. Eyes looked out from beneath a bony, protruding brow, giving the effect of gloom and brooding.

Beneath it writhed a four-legged reptilian beast, long and sinuous, its hind legs stretched out behind it catlike. Its beaked mouth opened as if it were part bird of prey.

At the bottom the artist had drawn in another physical anomaly. The body of this third animal was covered with a shell, but unlike any turtle Giles had ever seen. The legs were longer, slender, the body stout, the head similar to that of a dog, with large round ears pricked up as if listening to the susurration of desert wind against heated sand.

Giles folded the map and tucked it away. He would examine other beasts later. Now all he wanted to do was try to doze off as his *lirjan* perversely sought the rockiest part of the track.

The day wore on—and the desert stretched forever. Kasha disappeared behind the caravan, taking the ocean with it. For miles around, Giles saw only hard, flat soil. He supposed that the sand would come later. Surely, if this was a desert, then there must be sand.

He shaded his eyes with one hand to see into the heat-shimmered distance. Something broke the monotonous flatness through which the caravan passed. Small hills, eroded cliffs, perhaps. But the heat radiating off the land erased any detail. Giles could neither see clearly nor determine distances. It might be one league or ten to the cliffs.

Giles rocked back and forth on his *lirjan,* watching the bobbing heads of Keja and Petia ahead of him, falling into an almost hypnotic trance. The boy, Anji, was seated in front of Petia out of Giles' line of sight. He wondered idly if their backs ached as badly as his did. He was grateful when the caravan leader called a halt at midday.

Anji nimbly dropped to the hard ground to aid Petia, then hurried back to Keja's mount and helped the small thief. Giles was damned if a mere child was going to help him. After all, he was a veteran of twenty years at war and had seen and done everything—twice. He threw his foot over the *lirjan*'s withers and slid off. Pain shot through his legs. First the ankles, then the knee, and finally it reached his hips. He staggered back against the animal and heard it grumble. Turning, he grabbed a pack rope, hanging on while feeling came slowly back into his legs. Foolish, Giles, he thought. Next time he'd let the boy help.

The afternoon was much the same, although to the west Giles spied rounded sand dunes of beige and brown. The midday meal sat uneasily on his stomach as he endured the *lirjan*'s punishment well beyond the normal dinner time when the caravan master finally called a halt. Giles wanted only a light meal before the sandy horizon swallowed the sun.

Small fires burned around the perimeter of the camp, the *lirjan* tethered inside the circle of humans. The caravan master insisted on posting guards to watch for brigands; Giles said nothing about the Harifim. As nervous as the master appeared, he might put them out of the caravan at the slightest hint of impropriety on their part.

"Are you all right, Giles?" Petia asked.

"Just tired, Petia. I'm getting too old to take beatings. I'll be all right, unless I get more bright ideas." Giles snorted. "Can't imagine why I tried to take on all the Harifim by myself." But he did know why and it irritated him even more than the beating. Keja and Petia were so young, so agile. What did an old and tired soldier like himself have to offer? He remembered younger days and all he'd done then. There had been some good times interspersed with the stretches of bad, and he had tried to bring back those with a bit of derring-do. He had known Ryilla's men watched him; he had seen the eyes peeking through the tent. But he'd thought he could conquer all.

Just as Petia and Keja thought they could.

"My hip joints will never be the same." Petia laughed. "Want some tiffa? With sugar?"

"I've had enough for now. I'll just lie here and tell my ribs to quit hurting."

Returning to the small blaze, Petia sat cross-legged in front of it.

"Petia?" Keja looked at her for a time. "Why are you so aloof? We've been together for quite a while now, and you must know what sort of fellow I am. I need more than just simple companionship. I think you do, too."

She stared at him over the rim of her cup. "You've known too many others. I cannot look forward to being cast off like an unwanted garment. You see, Keja, I don't trust you. We are both thieves, but I don't think we have the same ethic, the same standard."

"Who are you to talk of ethic? Thieves have no ethic."

"Perhaps not. But this thief knows better than to become involved with another thief. And a Trans must be careful with humans. Do you think we have forgotten the Trans War? That any of us *can*?"

The Trans—magically created hybrids of human and animals—had been the result of a thwarted love affair between Lord Lophar of Trois Havres and the Lady Sorceress Cassia n'Kaan. He had used her cruelly, seeking only monetary gain. In her wrath she had cursed all his holdings, his vassals and serfs, and the man himself. The Trans, more animal than human in those days, had been imprisoned, reviled, enslaved. The decades-long Trans War had freed them, but it had done nothing to alleviate the prejudices many held against the human-animal hybrids.

"I don't care about the War," Keja said. "I care about you. And I care that at night my blankets are lonely."

"Ah, yes," Petia said. "Creature comforts. There's more to it than a moment's pleasure. But you wouldn't know that, would you?"

Keja lowered his head and glowered at the flames, his mouth set. He knew that if he spoke he would say something for which he would be sorry.

Anji snuggled next to Petia and pointed away to his left. A figure moved along the perimeter of the camp. Petia looked up from her cup. The caravan master strolled along, making small talk with the travelers.

Petia nudged Giles, who groaned and rubbed his eyes. "The caravan master?" he whispered. Anji nodded. Louder, Giles called, "Good evening, Master. A cup of tiffa at our fire?"

"What strange land do you hail from? I am the dhouti. No one calls me master. That is blasphemy against . . ." His voice trailed off. With an abrupt change of topic, he said, "I would like the tiffa. All well here?" The dhouti sank to his haunches and accepted a cup from Petia.

"As well as one might expect after a day of torture astride a *lirjan*, a beast unknown in our country."

The dhouti laughed and sipped loudly from his cup. "A ride one must be born to, I fear. You may become accustomed to it, but you will never be comfortable. You must be born of the desert."

"Then we have a long journey ahead of us. Can you offer advice?" Giles pulled the map from his tunic and spread it out before the dhouti. "I bought this in a shop in Kasha. The shopkeeper said that the routes shown are no longer used."

The dhouti leaned forward and studied the map, frowning. "Yes, that is true. An old map." He lifted his head and looked out into the desert night. "Forgotten cities there and there." He pointed to either side, but his fingers conveyed distances of many days journey.

"I'm curious about the old roads and the lost cities. Why are they no longer used?"

"Aaaah." A long sigh from the dhouti. "Dangerous. Dead cities inhabited by who knows what. Ghosts? Spirits? No commerce, no reason to use those ways. Nothing along those routes but abandoned cities, windows like empty sockets looking out at nothing." He shook his head. "Great cities once. Long, long ago. Nothing there now."

"What of these beasts illuminating the edge of the map? Are there stories about them? Legends?"

The dhouti pointed at the pictures with the short stick he carried for authority. "These? Yes, beasts of the desert. They exist out there in the places where men no longer travel."

Giles laughed. "We might be strangers to your land, but we know a joke."

"No jest. In the desert"—he flicked the tip of his stick over one shoulder—"beasts such as these still live. Perhaps they live in the forgotten cities. Good night, sirs and lady." He rose and thumped his thigh with the riding crop, then continued his rounds of the encampment.

For a long time Giles stared at the map with the animals marching in bizarre ranks around its borders. Finally he snorted, "Nonsense," and put the map away.

The days settled into a routine that consisted of endless sun, an endless track, the endless rocking of the *lirjan* beneath them. If the day brought a sameness, the nights were even more boringly identical. A plain meal, innumerable cups of strong tiffa, reading and writing lessons for Anji, Keja sulking, the dhouti making his rounds. The only positive change was that Giles recovered more each day from his beating.

For five days the *lirjan* followed one another like animals performing at a fair. Desert heat and the rocking motion and the animal's anus in front was all they could look forward to after a quick breakfast eaten standing. Giles finally understood the importance of much that the *lirjan* broker had insisted upon. If he had to ride along peering up an animal's backside, it had best be in good condition.

Keja became more sullen. He spoke little and seemed
only to be enduring the journey, withdrawing into himself,
cutting himself off from those around him. One evening
Petia tried to speak to him, but he turned and walked away
into the desert. Giles grumbled about this, wishing he could
have chosen his traveling companions as he'd done the
lirjan.

Soon enough Giles wished Keja's petulance and Petia's
anger at the small thief was all that he had to worry over.
The attack came at mid-morning of the sixth day. The
dhouti's sharp eyes centered on a swirl of dust on the
horizon. How he could distinguish the dust raised by riders
from that of a small dust devil, Giles would never know.
Shouts relayed from the front of the caravan to form a circle
as they did for the evening camp to keep the *lirjan* penned.

Initial confusion gave way to a methodical plan to defend
the caravan. It didn't surprise Giles that the caravaners had
experienced attacks before. They stayed on their animals,
facing outward to allow each rider enough space to wield
his sword.

Giles and Keja drew up on either side of Petia. "Get the
boy down," Giles yelled. "You'll need to be able to swing
your sword unhindered."

Anji slid off without a word and ducked behind the circle
of *lirjan.*

Keja pulled back the sleeve of his sword arm and,
throwing back his hood, tied a scarf around his head to keep
his sandy hair out of his eyes. Petia shifted nervously,
obviously worried more about Anji than herself. Giles said
nothing. He had faced too many battles not to know how to
prepare himself mentally. The old doubts rose; he forced
them away. His hand gripped firmly on the hilt of his sword.
Many had joined with him in battle; many had died. More
would this day. His confidence rose at the thought, at the
memories.

The dust cloud moved closer, an inexorable advance
dictated by fate. They saw the horses and their riders when
they came within half a league. At a hundred yards they saw
the drawn swords. The desert men swept by fifty yards
away, brandishing weapons and yelling vile insults. They
made no move to attack. They rode the complete circle one

time, as if showing their force to all sides of the caravan.

Petia muttered, "Why don't they attack? What are they waiting for?"

"You've never been in a battle before," Giles said grimly. "There's always a little game that takes place first. They're showing us how many they number, how swift they are, how well mounted. They are well outside the distance of a spear thrust or an arrow's accurate flight, although these people don't seem to use bows and arrows. So they are safe. They have the advantage and can take their time."

"And we just wait?"

"We can't attack. The *lirjan* are loaded, and they aren't fast enough to catch their horses. So, yes, we wait. We have no choice."

Keja shifted his weight. "Wouldn't it be better if you got behind us, Giles? You're not well enough to fight. You're still not healed."

"I've fought in worse shape than this."

The riders continued to circle, their cloaks flowing behind them like giant bats. They brandished their swords and howled maniacally in their desert tongue. It added to the eerie tension of the waiting.

One raider slowed his horse, certain of his own safety surrounded by his comrades. He studied each potential opponent as his mount danced daintily, hooves raking the air.

The rider—Giles decided he had to be the brigands' leader—stopped opposite them, made his decision and raised a long ululating call. Immediately the other riders wheeled and gathered behind for the attack.

The dhouti watched impassively from his seat atop his *lirjan*. When he heard the call, he raised his own cry and pointed. Giles and the others found themselves on the edge of a wedge pointing at the attackers.

"Wait," Giles protested, not wanting to be used as shock troops against the brigands.

"Attack or die, cowards!" came the warning from a grizzled old caravaner.

The riders moved forward slowly, gathering momentum like a boulder rolling downhill, then broke into a trot.

Turning to Keja and Petia, Giles called, "Go with the

attack. If we break rank now the entire caravan will be laid
open."

Giles saw Petia's lips move in the single name, "Anji."
Then the Trans let out a feline howl of rage and kicked her
animal forward. Keja found himself hard-pressed to keep
up with her, and Giles led the way on the right side of the
wedge.

The leader of the raiders raised high and stood in his
stirrups. He searched for something. When he didn't find it,
he veered off, racing at a tangent to the caravan circle. His
men swept after him and circled into the desert. They
slowed and the leader once again stared at the caravan,
searching.

Finally he halted and, standing in his stirrups, shouted,
"Dhouti." There followed a long statement in the desert
language directed to the caravan leader. When he had
finished the brief statement, the leader brandished his
sword once more and turned away, leading his band of
raiders into the desert.

The dhouti shouted, "Halt the attack! Halt, all halt!"
Giles reined in swiftly, but Keja had to grab Petia's sleeve
and almost tug her from the back of her animal before her
bloodlust quieted and common sense returned. She
couldn't follow and attack the brigands alone.

The defenders broke into a gabble as if they could not
believe their good fortune. They slapped one another on the
back and let out a shrill, rising cry that made Giles wince. It
was their way of proclaiming victory.

The dhouti rode slowly toward where Giles and the
others sat atop their mounts. Giles dropped his animal's
reins and slid to the ground. The dhouti squatted and
beckoned them to come over to him.

"What are you to the men of the desert?" he asked,
gazing coldly at them.

Giles lowered himself to sit cross-legged on the ground
opposite the dhouti. "We are nothing to them, as far as I
know. We arrived in Kasha less than two weeks ago. This is
our first trip into the desert, as you can plainly tell."

The dhouti's hand waved toward the vanishing cloud of
dust. "That is not what Seifal says. He says you seek
something in the desert that is not yours, that it will bring

your death. This foray was a warning. He could have cut my caravan to bits. What do you seek that upsets them so?" His face came nearer to Giles until they were eye to eye. "Do not lie to me. I will have your head if you do. I will send it to Seifal as a gift." His dark eyes did not blink.

Around him, Giles could hear the caravaners pulling the *lirjan* into position in the caravan once again, preparing to continue along their way.

"We look for the forgotten cities," Giles answered.

"And then?"

"We may find things discarded when the inhabitants left. Things that will be worth much in the markets of Kasha." Giles' gaze met the dhouti's unwaveringly. Keja and Petia stood to one side, listening.

"You lie," the dhouti said without emotion. "You seek a single object, yes? What is it? You may as well say, for I abandon you here, in any case."

Giles looked up at Keja and Petia, then turned back to the dhouti. "We seek the key to the Gate of Paradise."

"So. It is no wonder the Harifim attack. You walk into danger stupidly and with eyes open. My caravan will not be a part of it. We seek only safe passage to Kuilla. You will leave it here and now. I will give you some water and a compass. You have your own map. I wish you luck. Not in finding the key, may you be eternally cursed, but in keeping your lives." The dhouti rose and walked away.

By consigning them to the desert, he had sentenced them to a quick and painful death.

Chapter Six

"At least that mouse turd left us a waterskin." Giles hunkered down as he made a quick inventory of their supplies. He finally shook his head and sighed deeply. "It could have been worse. We won't starve or die of thirst—too soon."

"Always the optimist, eh, Giles?" Keja bounced around, filled with nervous energy. "What are we going to do in the middle of the desert? We don't know where we are, we have no protection. What if those raiders come back?"

"We do know where we are." Giles pointed to the track ahead and behind. Worn smooth by thousands of *lirjan* passing along it for more than a hundred years, it lay exposed for any eye to see. "We can follow it back to Kasha or ahead to Kuilla. There is some danger in staying on the caravan track but probably less than if we take out across the desert. At least we won't get lost."

Petia sat down on the ground and Anji squatted beside her. She looked at the two men. "You might as well sit down, too. It's time to make another decision. Do we go ahead or do we return to Kasha and give up the search for the key?" She handed the compass to Giles.

Giles sat down; Keja continued to pace.

"I didn't count on being abandoned in the middle of a desert, Giles." Keja's swarthy face flushed and his expression was bleak.

"Neither did I." Giles looked from Anji to Petia. "And you have the boy to think of, too."

"The boy will be all right," she said defensively. "He knows more about this country than we do. I'm more concerned with us. Can we survive out here?"

"We survived near drowning in the Flame Sorceress' cave in Trois Havres," Giles said. "Can we survive this heat? We

66

have supplies for ourselves and the animals. We have water, thanks to the dhouti. How long it will last is hard to say. The central question to answer is: how badly do we want the key?"

"I'm not ready to give up yet," Petia said quietly.

"Nor am I. How about you, Keja?"

Keja stared up toward the glowing sun and shook his fist. He looked at the other two. "You're going to have to blame quitting on someone else. I'll stay." He grinned, teeth flashing in the sunlight. "But I reserve the right to grumble."

"All right." Giles pulled out the map. "Let's see if we can figure out where we are."

A half hour later Giles felt more confident. He knew approximately where they were. If they continued along the caravan track for several more days, they should arrive at the place where Giles had planned to leave the caravan —the crossroads of an eastern caravan road to Masser.

When they gathered the reins of their *lirjan,* they could still see evidence of the caravan ahead of them. To either side the desert was empty, but ahead of them the dust drifted upward and to the east.

"Anyone averse to walking?" Giles asked. "It'll be easier on the animals and may save water. We're not in a hurry, anyway, are we?"

They tugged on the reins and the *lirjan* seemed startled that they were not being ridden. The track was wide enough for two animals, and at first Giles and Keja walked together as Petia and Anji followed. They talked little, reserving their strength. Still, it felt good having someone to walk with. For Giles it brought back the days during the Trans War and the comradeship in the ranks.

His mouth turned even drier when he remembered that, with the camaraderie, had come sudden, messy death.

The days settled into the monotony of rising with the sun, leading the animals through the day, and camping in the evening. They conserved their supplies, grudgingly became accustomed to the heat and began to feel more comfortable with the desert. But occasional strange occurrences kept them on edge. At times during the day, they heard eerie, unidentifiable sounds.

"There, there it is again!" Keja grated out. He wiped sand off his chapped lips. "The sound." He shuddered.

"It's just the wind whistling through rocks," Petia said. No one contradicted her, though the wind was deathly still.

At night the sounds came more frequently. Even Giles began to fidget and glance over his shoulder—only to find the same barren expanse that lay in front. Empty, silent and giving no clue to the source of the sounds. At times the moans were like human voices, lost souls, tormented beasts. At other times they were unlike any sound that they had ever heard.

Giles and the others grew more apprehensive, seemingly surrounded by something unseen. Giles feared that they would be attacked by the Harifim.

"What can we do about it?" Petia asked.

"I don't know. Nothing. We're committed to going on," Giles replied.

Anji spoke up. "Why not travel to one side of the caravan track? The going will not be as easy, but if the Harifim raiders come again they will expect to find us on the track."

"We'll have to go far off it," Giles said, considering the idea. He had wanted to stay with the easy path but, if the Harifim were responsible for the eerie sounds echoing across the bleak desert, leaving the track might confuse them. "We don't want to get lost, but it's worth a try." Even though Giles didn't admit it, he wanted to be free of the mournful sighs as much as Keja.

Giles scouted ahead, keeping to one side of the track. The small company followed, feeling more secure—and free of the inhuman cries for the moment.

The terrain changed and forced them back to the beaten track, sand dunes stretching like chains across the desert. Standing at the top of a tall dune, they observed an immense bleak plain, too long and wide to be called a canyon, stretching as far as the eye could see. Columns of jagged stone thrust up from the floor like tributes to long-dead heroes, and boulders the size of small sailing ships littered the plain, turning sleek, wind-driven sand into a virtually impassable expanse.

In its grim fashion, the scene inspired wonder—and fear. It nearly broke the travelers' courage.

Anji spoke. "It is said that the gods made the desert for themselves. No one else could love it, so they alone could frolic here."

To that, not even Keja had a comment.

Evening was upon them by the time they reached the rocky floor of the plain. It had become increasingly hotter as they descended, and the boulders that littered the plain were immense, towering over them and their animals. Tired in body and numbed in soul by the overpowering landscape, they tethered the *lirjan* and dropped thankfully into the shade. Night was spent listening apprehensively for distant howls and moans.

The disturbing cries came just before sunrise, then died out, as if vanishing in the forlorn distance.

Just after the sun poked its diffuse, bleary red eye over the rocky horizon, they encountered cold even more severe than they had felt in the high desert. They ate quickly, stamping their feet about the fire, anxious to be on their way and to have their blood circulating once again through sluggish veins.

Keja let out a roar when he went to pack his *lirjan*. "Who's the prankster?" he demanded, dark eyes darting from Giles to Petia and then back.

Supplies were strewn over a thirty foot circle. Keja's belongings had been dumped on the ground, his bag flat and empty near the head of his somnolent *lirjan*.

"We wouldn't do anything like that, Keja. This journey is difficult enough without causing trouble for one another." Petia studied the scattered goods, then looked at Anji. "You didn't do this, did you?"

"Oh, no, Mistress. It is the djinn's handiwork."

"You don't believe in those tales, do you, Anji?" Giles said.

"Oh, yes. There are djinn in the desert. Ifrit, too. But the djinn are the ones who would do this. They like to make tricks. I have heard so many times."

"Who are the djinn?" Keja asked, puzzled. "Not more of the Harifim?"

"They are spirits," Anji said, his voice taking on an almost reverent tone. "They live in the rocks. Up in the hills. They frighten people and would think this a funny prank. It makes extra work for you. They watch—and laugh to themselves while you curse."

"I don't believe that. I don't believe in spirits. Come on, help me gather this stuff up and get it packed."

Anji bobbed his head and ran off to begin gathering grain sacks and the other items scattered about. Petia shook her head and went to fetch her own pack. Her cry of dismay brought the others at a run. They stared at the pack ropes.

The previous evening she had coiled them carefully and set them on an outcropping of a boulder, where they would be near to hand. Instead of a neat coil, the ropes were now tied in knot after knot, more than a hundred knots in the thirty-foot length. While they were simple overhand knots, not difficult to untie, the chore proved time-consuming and frustrating.

Giles looked at Anji. The boy solemnly said, "Djinn. They are very good at this sort of devilment. There are many stories. Some must hold kernels of truth."

Expecting to find some trick had also been played on him, Giles searched his own gear. He found nothing amiss but had the feeling that it was only a matter of time before his turn came.

When they were finally able to begin picking their way through the rocky plains, Giles called Anji to his side. "Is there anything we can do to placate the djinn?" he asked.

The boy looked up at him. "I do not know what 'placate' means."

"Is there anything we can do so the djinn won't play these tricks? Can we leave something for them? Some food, water, a present? If they do this every night, we'll be ripping out each other's throats."

"The stories don't say anything about how to satisfy the djinn," the boy said. "It is their sense of humor. They do it for fun, not for gain." Anji's foot scuffed at a rock in the middle of a faint track. "Maybe we will get beyond where they live," he said.

"If they really are spirits," Giles said, "distances won't

make any difference. They can come and go whenever they wish, and as far as they wish. I hope they tire of this quickly."

Anji said nothing more, drifting back to walk beside Petia and leaving Giles to worry about the djinn. He hardly noticed the strange electric tension in the air, the odd stillness or the reddening of the sky until in mid-afternoon the first sand storm struck with paralyzing virulence.

"Hurry," Giles yelled as the first light, grainy touch of the storm cut at his face. "Cover the animals' heads with your cloaks so they can breathe, then pull your own cowls up over your heads and get down behind your *lirjan* on the side opposite the storm."

The wind blew stronger, the slashing sand hitting with the impact of a hammer blow, stinging their bare hands and faces by the time they had the animals down. Anji was everywhere, encouraging with his soft voice, as if he had dealt with animals all his young life.

They had barely crawled behind the *lirjan,* hiding their heads, when the storm hit with its full force. The once-clear sky filled with red sand and choking dust, blowing northward across the plain. Keja winced as it filtered into the folds of his garment, piling up in a small, irritating ridge along his neck. He wanted desperately to raise his head and shake the dirt off, but he knew the penalty if he did. This only irritated; movement would slice his skin. He kept his head down and his eyes squeezed shut tightly.

They heard the wind blowing, the heavier grains of sand hitting against their cowls. Petia felt sorry for the animals, even though she knew their shaggy coats and thick skins probably felt little of the storm. As long as their eyes and noses were covered, they would come through the storm unscathed.

After more than an hour, the storm passed. At first, they hardly ventured a glance out for fear that it was a trick of the storm designed to lure them from safety, but cramped muscles and burning, reddened skin finally forced them to take a peek.

"We got through it," Petia said, amazed, "and it's over." Then despair took control. "Everything is against us. Even

the weather. We can't go on. We'll die!" Her body sleekened
as she adopted catlike features unconsciously to combat the
danger she faced.

"Please," Keja said. "Let's not get hysterical." His own
voice carried a brittle edge of terror that Giles had heard
before. Soldiers nearing the limits of their endurance struck
out at others, just as Keja was doing with Petia.

"Petia, tend the *lirjan*. Keja, check to see if any of the
ropes have loosened. We don't want our supplies being left
over half the desert. Anji, scout the ridge. Tell me of the
storm's track." His firmness and no-nonsense commands
broke the impending flare-ups. They shook their clothing
out, uncovered the animals' heads and helped them onto
their feet. They were soon laughing aloud as they watched
the *lirjan* make their skin quiver from head to tail. The fine,
gritty dust billowed out of their coats, forcing the humans
to back away before it got into their eyes.

Their mood lighter, they started once more along the
compass heading dictated by Giles. The faint signs of a
track beneath their animals' hooves spurred them on; even
the diabolical storm and its load of dust hadn't been able to
obliterate the path.

But their lightheartedness didn't long endure. The storm
was only the first of many—and the ones following were
even more brutal. For the next four days they were harried
by dust devils, whirlwinds and two more savage sand
storms.

"Someone wants us to turn back," Petia said. "They send
the storms to kill us."

"Nonsense. It's just the seasonal weather in this lovely
desert," Keja said, his tone mocking. "These things would
occur whether we were here or not."

They traveled cautiously, eyes darting back and forth
along the rocky horizon seeking out new indications of
storm. They saw nothing. Keja began relaxing and even
managed to drift off to a fitful sleep astride his *lirjan*. Only
when a rock grazed his forehead, almost knocking him off,
did he come awake again.

His hand shot up to a spot just under his sandy hairline
and came away bloody. "By all the gods," Keja muttered,

his eyes hardening as he twisted around to confront his attacker.

Giles looked up sharply from his position at the head of the ragged column. "What did you say?"

"A djinn just attacked me."

Giles studied Keja's face for a moment. "Tell us about it," he said.

"Not much to tell. I was dozing and he threw a stone at me." Keja held up his stained fingers; the scalp wound already had begun to clot over. "He must have followed us for quite a distance, off to one side, to our left. After he threw the rock, he pranced along, making faces at me, then made an obscene gesture and disappeared."

"I see," Giles said carefully. "Did you take your ration of water or did you try to leave it for Petia?"

"Giles," Keja said in exasperation. "I'm all right. I . . . never mind. I should have known you wouldn't believe me. The sun *hasn't* gotten to me."

Petia broke in. "Don't be stupid, Keja. Giles just wanted to make sure—"

"So now I'm stupid. First I'm a liar, and now stupid." Keja yanked the halter of his *lirjan* and stalked ahead of the others.

Leaning over, Giles took Petia's upper arm and squeezed, cautioning her to silence. "It's the heat," he told her. "I saw it during the War. Stress, hardship, they do strange things to the mind. When we can rest, Keja will be just fine."

"Giles!" protested the woman. "*I* believe Keja. *I* think he saw a djinn, if he says so." She snapped the reins and rode off in unconscious mimicry of Keja.

Giles stopped and stared, not knowing what to make of it. They were all going crazy from the heat. All of them, including himself.

Keja stayed ahead of them until Giles called for him to halt for a rest. He accepted the cup of water from Petia without looking at her. He sipped, staring off into the distance, and handed it back to her.

"Look, Keja. I'm sorry. It slipped out. I didn't mean it that way."

"Yes, everything just seems to slip out and not be meant

lately," Keja sneered. "I'm tired of always being the dolt. In the Flame Sorceress' cave it was me who had to be rescued. It's foolish Keja Tchurak who thinks he sees rock-throwing djinn. I should forget this insane quest and head back for Kasha."

Giles settled to the ground in the shade of a large boulder. He wiped the perspiration from his forehead. "I think it's time to talk this out," he said, gesturing for the others to sit.

He gazed up at the cloudless azure sky while Petia and Keja settled down. Anji sat to one side, his back against a boulder, and closed his eyes. Giles decided Anji neither cared nor understood what was going on. To the slave boy, nothing mattered.

"It's the heat," Giles said. "Sand storms, whirlwinds. It's getting on everyone's nerves. Petia's remark wasn't intentional, but we're all starting to bicker." He studied Petia and Keja to see how they were taking this. Not well, he decided. "It's getting to us. We are in an unfamiliar land, alone. We're our own company, our only company—and it will get worse if we don't take care. We need to remind ourselves why we're here. We didn't have too many problems getting the third key. Maybe it was too easy."

"It wasn't that easy," Petia said. "But it took only a few days once we found the sorceress' cave. We've just been on the road too long. And it's dusty," she finished with distaste. She made unconscious preening motions on whiskers that weren't there.

"That's it," Giles agreed. "We're almost to the crossroad where the old track heads east for Masser. We'd better decide now if we want to go on with this. Once we turn east," he warned, "we're committed. Why don't we find a good place to camp near here and rest for a day? Then we can talk about it again. Meanwhile each of us should think about it. We'll decide later, after we're rested."

"We know the track back to Kasha," Petia said, glancing over to where Anji slept. "We don't know what's ahead."

"You want to quit?" Keja asked testily. "Is that what you want?"

"No, it's only something to think about." Petia folded her arms tightly around herself, withdrawing.

The djinn had not given up. Now that the four travelers had settled in for a night's sleep, the djinn cavorted and danced in tight, vaporous circles; the humans had arrived for their entertainment. When slow, deep snores reached the djinn, they locked thin arms and drifted downward into the camp. Their misty fingers trailed over Keja's forehead wound, into Giles' nose, making him sneeze, to Petia's more intimate spots and provoking a nasty hiss more catlike than human. The djinn even fastened insubstantial fingers around Anji's wrists, pinning him and bringing back memories of chains and cages.

But these were only fleeting amusements. Barely able to contain their mirth, they whispered off to put out the fire that Giles had carefully built, threw sand in the barley soup, untied one *lirjan* and hid it among the boulders and, finally, as the crowning insult, spilled the contents of Giles' pack.

They had saved him to build the dread and apprehension; he now became the victim of the same pranks that Keja and Petia had suffered earlier.

Only then did the djinn retreat to congregate along one rocky ridge and discuss further pranks and relive the marvelous ones they had just perpetrated.

Giles sneezed again and peered out through one bleary eye when laughter floated down to him. Groaning, he sat up and fixed the fire, wondering how it had gone out. He fell back asleep, even louder laughter echoing in his head, as much dreamlike as real.

"Now do you believe me?" Keja asked smugly.

"We believe, we believe," Giles said, pushing the dried dung back into the fire. "Malicious, aren't they?"

Petia spat out the first mouthful of barley soup she tried. The sand choked her. "Will we ever be rid of them? Or will they only get worse?"

Giles leaned forward, pulling out the map and fastening down the corners with small rocks. His expression made Petia ask, "What's wrong, Giles?"

"Maybe nothing. I just wondered, since the djinn are real, if the rest of these creatures might not be real, too. After all, the dhouti did warn us about them."

The rest, in spite of the djinn's pranks, did them all good. After they packed the animals on the second morning, Giles said, "It's time for decisions. Are we going forward or back? Into more djinn—and other beasts—or do we retreat?"

The way Giles spoke revealed his decision: push on. They didn't even bother to sit down for the last round of discussion. Petia tugged at a pack knot to make certain it was tight. She cupped her hands for Anji's foot, boosting him onto the *lirjan.* "Might as well go on," she said without turning her head.

Keja looked briefly at Giles. "Any second thoughts?" he asked. "Is the key to the Gate of Paradise worth the risk?"

Giles' weathered face turned impassive and hid his true thoughts. For a man whose joints ached more with every new day, passing through that Gate and into Paradise was worth any risk. So what if he died trying to retrieve the keys? He had no life other than the quest. Giles allowed himself a small smile now. If anything, this hunt gave purpose to his life, and being with Petia and Keja wasn't too bad.

Even watching after the boy hadn't proved as onerous as he'd thought it would be. Giles Grimsmate enjoyed life more now than he had since the end of the War.

Giles nodded. "What about you, Keja?"

"Doesn't make any difference, does it? Two for going on."

Petia scowled. "That's not fair, Keja. We want your decision. We don't want to hear later how you were out-voted. Tell us what you think."

"I think we should go on, too. I think the only ones having any fun on this trip are the djinn. And maybe Anji, who seems to have more energy than the rest of us put together." He winked at the boy, who blushed and averted his gaze as befitting a slave being spoken of in the presence of masters.

"I am enjoying this trip very much, Master Keja. I have regular meals, new clothes, an adventure in the desert, where I have never been, and a new mistress who is most kind and who pretends she has freed me. I will go where she goes." He looked shyly at Petia.

"We'll have no more of 'master' and 'mistress,' Anji. I

am Petia and you know their names are Giles and Keja. Call us by our names. We are not your owners. You are free, you may leave us whenever you wish. I told you that in Kasha." She turned toward Giles. "Are we going to stay here all day?"

They had decided. The three gathered their reins and headed into the sun, which rose as hot as on previous days, the dust as dry and the effort as tiring. But somehow the mood of the small company had lifted. They found the energy to make small talk and to occasionally joke.

The caravan road that had once crossed the track from Kasha to Kuilla was plainly marked by a tall cairn looming in the shimmering distance. When they arrived they found that the spire towered several times the height of a person. On top sat four *lirjan* skulls, bleached by the sun, staring sightlessly in the four directions of the compass.

"Someone's grim idea of humor," Keja muttered.

"Just the reality of the desert," Giles said.

They paused only briefly at the cairn. There were no signposts, and they turned eastward after Giles had examined his map once again.

"For someone who could memorize a map of the coast of Bandanarra, you certainly refer to that map a lot," Petia said shortly, the heat beginning to wear on her again.

"Into the unknown," Giles said, folding the map. "Can you imagine how your homeland has changed in a hundred years?"

"A lot more than this country has changed, you can be sure," Petia replied. "The Trans War made sure of that."

A somber mood settled on them as they turned east from the main track. More than once they turned to look back at the cairn dwindling from their sight. When they could no longer see it, they faced steadily eastward, and settled into their own thoughts. Giles nervously fingered the cloth beneath which the map rode easily. They had left the only place where any possibility of seeing humans existed. They had made the turn, the decision.

They were truly alone in the desert.

Chapter Seven

The terrain began to change within a few miles as they proceeded down the Track of Fourteen indicated on Giles' map. Their *lirjan*'s hooves crunched differently, revealing less sand and a more solid ground. Before they knew it, they were walking on a wasteland of solid granite. The large boulders that had plagued their passage gave way to fantastic formations of wind-carved rock looming above them. Shadows created canyons of dancing darkness and light, yet the coolness they expected never quite made its presence known. If anything, this bizarre land of lacy rock sculptings and impossibly hard ground was hotter than the desert sand ever had been.

"Look," said Giles, pointing. Petia and Keja said nothing. Anji still rode a pack animal, fitfully sleeping. Giles decided it was just as well that the child didn't see the mummified corpses of *lirjan*, desiccated vestiges of failed caravans long past. Occasionally Giles saw packs and other remnants of the baggage that had been transported great distances to end up at this lonely, death-filled spot. Most were empty shells from which the goods had long been removed. Perhaps the caravaners had redistributed the goods, or animals had carried off foodstuffs, leaving only empty cloth.

Probably the caravaners had died and desert scavengers had done the looting.

Throughout the morning, the companions kept a sharp lookout. By the midday break, their eyes ached from sand, heat and the twisting patterns of light and darkness playing against the rock formations. They sat, knuckling their eyes.

Keja was the first to put feelings into words. "I don't care if we're attacked or not, I'm closing my eyes. The glare is killing them."

"Put some water on a cloth and hold it against them," Giles said. "That will help some. I'll keep watch."

Giles wandered away, seeking shadow, hoping to find some small oasis of coolness. He knew it had to be degrees cooler in the shadows, but it was not a noticeable difference from the heat reflected off the stony sculptings.

Ahead Giles saw more mummified *lirjan*. He had become accustomed to finding them along the Track of Fourteen. Lying beside the bleached bones were two humans, dead for many years, mummified by the preternaturally dry heat. The packs, still roped to the *lirjan*, caught Giles' eye. They contained the caravaners' cargo.

Giles bent over the dead animal and cut the ropes with his dagger. The pack rolled slightly, allowing him to pull open the cover and reveal a mound of desert garments, fine weaves unravaged by time's hot, groping fingers. A long, slender bundle, wrapped in a kind of canvas and tied with dried tendons, attracted his attention. He lifted it from the pack and cut the ties. The stiff canvas fought back as he unwrapped the heavy bundle.

He let out a low whistle of appreciation for the swords he found. The highly polished blades betrayed not a speck of rust. The hilts were of beautiful workmanship, joining the blades as if forged from a single piece of steel, the finest steel Giles had ever seen.

"Amazing workmanship," he said, barely allowing himself more than a reverent whisper. "And there are five! Never have I seen one sword this fine, and I stumble across five!"

Picking them up, one by one, he examined them closely. Four were nearly alike, the only differences in the decorations adorning the hilts. The fifth sword had a florid inscription beautifully engraved on the blade near the hilt. He brought the sword closer, attempting to read the script. The language was not familiar.

He rewrapped the swords and pawed through the pack. He found only more clothing. The others could look at it before they went on. He carried the bundle of swords back to his *lirjan* and slid it under the ropes holding his supplies.

"What did you find, Giles?" asked Petia. "Anything to

make the glare go away?"

"Intriguing goods on yon pack animal," he said. "Good clothing still in the pack farthest from here. Go and see if you want anything from it while I take care of this blinding light."

"The glare first, then the looting," said Keja, squinting.

Giles nodded and began carving slits in small, flat pieces of bone he'd picked up from the *lirjan* skeleton. He unraveled some thread and tied it to a pair of bones with the thin slits carved in them. He tossed one set over to Keja.

"Try these." Giles watched as Keja fastened the thread around his head. His eyesockets took on the aspect of a death's skull, showing only bone white with a tiny black slit running the length of each. "Well? Do they work?"

"I can't see too well," Keja said, "but they do reduce the glare."

"Over the span of a few days, your eyes will adjust to the narrowed field of vision—and with the glare cut down, you won't be complaining so much." Giles went ahead and fashioned the sun slits for Petia and Anji, then finished with a set for himself.

They looked like eerie, blind creatures risen from the grave, but their vision cleared. Before the end of the day, they discovered one additional benefit. The slit prevented blowing dust from caking their eyelids shut.

That evening Giles piled dried animal dung on the fire and huddled closer. Coming with the typical desert cold was a strong, gusty wind.

Across his lap he held the wrapped bundle of swords. "A present for you," he said to the others.

"I wondered if you were going to share this fine booty, whatever it is," Keja said. "I saw you hide the package on your *lirjan*."

"No holding back, remember? We're partners, even if we don't trust one another overly much." Giles began to unwrap the bundle. Petia and Anji moved closer to him in anticipation. Giles enjoyed the suspense. It reminded him of the solstice celebrations in his village, the gift giving, the anticipation of youth for what they might receive.

When he finally revealed the blades, which flashed in the firelight, the others murmured in appreciation. Anji audibly caught his breath. "The swordmakers of Hamri," he whispered in awe.

"What of these, Anji?" Giles asked.

"I have seen two such swords in the market in Kasha. One cannot mistake the workmanship, Master Giles. They are most expensive. Hamri was a place far to the east, on the coast, I think. Very famous swordmakers. But the town is gone, destroyed because of the evil that lived there, it is said. There are no more swords of this quality. See."

He pointed to a small mark below the hilt. "The mark of the Hamri swordmakers. The little symbol to the right is the signature of the master craftsman who made the sword. Very expensive—priceless! They are said to be brave in battle, such swords."

Giles lifted one sword and handed it to Keja. He gave a second to Petia. "See how they feel."

The two rose and hefted the weight of the new weapons, going through both offensive and defensive movements with them, parrying, lunging, twisting and turning in mock battle. The ring of steel on steel was more than musical—it created a symphony that brought a tiny tear to Giles' eyes. Never had he heard or seen such perfection. Keja was the first to return to the fire.

"Incredible, Giles. It's as if it were made for me. Beautifully balanced."

Petia handed her sword back to Giles. "May I try another? This one is too heavy."

Giles handed her the shortest of the five. It took only a moment for Petia to know that this sword was better for her. She smiled and ran her fingers along the blade. "A nice find, Giles. Thank you."

"I've reserved one for myself." He lifted the sword with the intricate inscription on the blade. "I don't know if it's right for my style or not, but such beauty appeals to me." He rose to test it. Never had the old warrior experienced such fluidity with a blade; it made him feel years younger wielding such a finely tempered weapon.

He, too, rubbed his thumb along the edge of the blade, testing its sharpness. Giles bent closer, examining the delicate script near the hilt, fingertip tracing the fine engraving.

The blade leaped in his hand as if the sword assumed a life of its own. He felt a vibration of energy run through his hand and up his arm, giving a power he had not felt even during his prime. He staggered to his feet, clutching the sword as if it might escape. An aura of the purest blue surrounded the blade, shimmering as if heat radiated from the steel.

Giles wondered if he should throw down the sword. Moving his left hand toward the blade, he felt the energy. Then his common sense took hold and he touched the script once more with his forefinger. The sword's radiance vanished instantly. For a brief moment, it lingered in his hand and arm, then it, too, was gone. All that was left was a slight odor of ozone.

Giles sat down by the fire once again. The others stared at him curiously.

"What was it, Giles?" Keja asked. "Did you hear something?" He leaned forward, a concerned look on his face.

"You couldn't see?" Giles asked. Their puzzled expressions gave him answer enough. "The blade came alive when I touched the script. Let me try it again, now that I'm prepared."

Giles held the sword in his right hand and touched the script once more. Again he felt the vibration, heard the angry buzz. He held the sword in front of Petia and Keja. "Can't you see the energy shimmering off the edge of the blade?"

"No."

He thumbed the script again, then held the sword out to Petia. "Feel normal?"

"Yes, a little heavier than I like," she answered.

"All right, now touch the script with your finger."

Petia touched the letters, stared uncomprehendingly at the blade, then touched them again. Wordlessly, she handed the sword on to Keja. His reaction was much the same.

"Did you feel it?" Giles asked. "It's like a . . . it's magic! You can feel the energy of the sword. I have no idea what it will do in combat, but it makes me want to find out." Giles sobered and shook his head. "It's been years since I said anything like that. Wanting to go into battle." He shivered in reaction, but the feeling lingered within his breast. The sword *was* magical. He knew it.

"Keep that sword for yourself," Keja said. "I don't like the feel of it, not at all."

"I'll be careful until I find out exactly what it can do," Giles said as he placed it back into the bundle. He had been raised with stories of youth stumbling across weapons too powerful for their hand and of the dire consequences of their misuse. Being too cautious with this fine sword didn't seem possible.

Giles drifted off to sleep, his hand resting on the wrapped sword.

The days marched stolidly, one after another. The Track of Fourteen wound its way out of the monstrous sandstone formations and into another plain, this one dotted with boulders and knee-high *raska* bushes, which provided their *lirjan* with succulent green leaves.

Almost hypnotized by the terrain, it took several seconds for any of them to realize that the odd noise carrying over the plain had to be running footsteps. By the time they had turned on their mounts, a beast had reached the rearmost *lirjan*. Twisting its tail, it pulled the caravan animal off its feet, spilling Petia and Anji onto the desert floor. The slavering, long-fanged beast loomed over them, taloned claws tentatively groping for the helpless pair.

Without bothering to stop his mount, Giles slid to the ground. He ran, tugging at the new sword, which now hung in the scabbard at his side. It slid forth easily. He thumbed the inscription, feeling the thrum of energy.

The beast's taloned paws flashed down toward Petia and Anji. It stood on legs as massive as stumps, planted wide apart. A mane of red hair billowed around its neck and flowed down its back.

Giles saw he would be too late; his legs couldn't pump fast enough to give him the speed needed. *"Aieeee!"* he shrieked, the old battle-lust rising within him. All thought of personal injury, of aching joints, of anything but saving Petia and Anji fled his mind.

The beast turned and faced the oncoming man. It was weaponless; with those teeth and talons it didn't need more.

Giles raised the sword and swept forward like a human

tornado swathed in steel. Keja followed a dozen steps back, approaching cautiously, waiting to see what developed between Giles and the beast.

The beast backed away from Giles' insane blood-crazed rush. As Giles slashed, it dodged to one side with a speed that belied its size. It scrabbled in the sand with taloned hands, as if searching for something. It picked up a stone, then stood, facing Giles.

Giles dropped *en garde.* "Come and throw yourself on my sword tip, monster," he snarled. He didn't care if it understood him or not. The beast backed away, glancing to see where the others were. Without warning, it raised the jagged stone and charged at the man. Giles extended the sword and waited for the charging creature to run onto it. As the beast reached Giles, it skipped athletically to one side and threw the stone at Giles.

Giles was caught by surprise. In his experience, no animal—save man—moved laterally with such quickness. The stone grazed his head, staggering him. He saw that the beast had stopped to pick up another stone and charged when the hairy creature bent over.

Giles' sword caught the beast in the shoulder as it straightened, a new stone in taloned hand. The beast staggered. Blood oozed from the wound, and its thick body trembled. It shivered, tried to clap a hand to the wound, and fell to knobby knees.

Petia had struggled to her feet and reached Giles' side, her sword ready. They stood, waiting, for a new attack, but the beast sagged. It attempted to stand, lifted one knee off the ground but wasn't able to get any farther. Tremors ran through its body.

"It's had it," Keja cried, taking his place alongside the other two. Anji had gathered an armload of *lirjan* chips, and danced around, pelting the kneeling beast with the clods.

Keja started forward to administer the killing thrust when the beast muttered, "I surrender." One hand lifted weakly as if to ward off Keja. "I surrender."

"It can talk," Keja whispered. The small thief took a step backward, the tip of his sword dipping.

"So it seems." Giles went to the beast, put his hand under

the beast's elbow, and helped the creature to its feet. "Keja, get a fire started, so we can boil some water. Petia, something for bandages. We can't let him bleed to death."

"Why not?" demanded Keja. "He tried to kill us. Slay him now!"

Giles grabbed Keja's wrist and stopped the lunge. "Let's talk to him first, then decide," Giles said, a snap of command in his words. With ill grace, Keja backed off.

When the beast's wound had been attended, and mugs of tea had been made from the last of the boiling water, Giles lowered himself to the ground, facing the beast. "Now, tell us who you are and why you attacked us."

The beast peered at them nearsightedly. "I thought you were skeleton men. I hate the skeleton men and their lord."

"Do you mean skeleton men come out here into the desert?" Giles and the others exchanged puzzled looks.

"You know of the skeleton men, too?" the beast asked.

"Two were pointed out to us in Kasha. Do they live out here?"

The beast nodded. "In Shahal." He gestured eastward with this head.

"What is Shahal?" Petia asked.

Anji spoke up. "A lost city in the desert."

"It's not lost," the beast said, looking oddly docile now that he wasn't attacking. "I know exactly where it is."

Anji drew himself up proudly. "In Kasha they say that Shahal is a lost city."

The beast stared at Anji. His myopic, unwavering eyes disconcerted the boy, who finally looked away into the dust.

"The city is not lost. How can it be when I know it is many days travel to the east. It was my home . . . once." The beast paused and stared off into the distance, remembering better days. "It was the home of many beasts, a magnificent rock city, Shahal. Cool during the day, pleasant in the evening when we could look across the desert from our balconies and watch the setting sun." Sadness and nostalgia tinged his voice—and bitterness.

"You said it *was* your home," Keja said. "Why isn't it your home any longer?"

"The Skeleton Lord stole it from us. He and his army of skeleton warriors. They outnumbered us. And the skeleton beings are difficult to kill. They have no blood, they did not bleed when we fought them; they kept coming. We were driven out and the Skeleton Lord took our city for his own evil purposes."

"What did you do then?" Giles asked.

"We scattered into the desert. When we tried to go back, we were turned away by the skeleton men."

Giles pulled the map from his tunic. "There is no city named Shahal on this map." He leaned forward and placed his finger on the map. "This is where we are now."

The beast grabbed the map away and held it closer to his face. "Look, look," he cried. "My friends. See, these are my friends!"

The three bent forward to look. The beast's head came up and he looked from one to another. "My friends, these are my friends. We lived together in Shahal." He rocked back and forth with obvious delight.

Keja nodded his head. "So much for your imaginary beasts, Giles. Just legends, isn't that what you said?"

Giles grimaced in response. "These are your friends?" he asked the beast. "You know them?" He pointed to the edge of the map.

"Yes, I know them all. There are others. But nobody believes in us anymore." Giles thought the beast was going to start crying, but the redhaired monstrosity stopped just short of it.

"Do you know where the others are?" Petia asked. "Where you can find them?"

The beast turned his hands palm up and gestured into the desert. "They live many places. Like me. In the desert."

Petia turned to Giles and Keja. "Perhaps we could make an alliance with them. We'll need help if we are going up against this Skeleton Lord."

"Of course," Keja said. "We've been attacked by one of these beasts. Now you want them for friends. Sometimes I don't understand you, Petia."

"I don't understand you, either. Look, the beast thought we were the Skeleton Lord's minions. Is it any wonder he attacked us? You remember what the skeleton men were like." She turned to the beast, putting her hand on its forearm. "Could you find your friends and bring them to us?"

"Petia, I think we ought to consider what you're suggesting," Giles said cautiously.

"Really, Giles, what is there to consider? If we are going to Shahal, we are going to have to fight the skeleton men and their lord. We are going to need help. The beasts can help. Perhaps we can even give them their city back." She concentrated, sweat pouring down her face. At times she could touch the thoughts—the emotions—of others. She did so now, linking lightly with the beast. Only honesty and a simple-minded friendliness came forth.

If nothing else, Petia felt a bond with the beast, her own Trans nature being closer to the mangy creature than either Giles' or Keja's.

A frown wrinkled the beast's face as he listened. It vanished slowly as the impact of what Petia had said became clear to him. "Give us our city back?" he said, obviously startled at this new idea.

"No promises," Giles said hastily. "We don't even know if we can get to the city. Would your friends be willing to help?"

"Oh, yes, I'm certain of it. I'll go now and bring them." The beast started to rise.

Petia held him back. "You are wounded. Another day of rest before you go. There's no hurry."

The beast lay back, beaming in satisfaction. That pleased Petia, and she felt vindicated in her judgment of the beast.

"Again?" asked Petia, frustration at a peak. She vowed to pronounce the beast's name, but when he voiced it for what must have been the hundredth time, Petia knew she'd never be able to repeat it.

"Red Mane will have to do," said Giles. To Red Mane, he said, "You're healed enough to fetch back the others." He ventured a small pat on the beast's hairy shoulder. Red Mane smiled, fangs gleaming wickedly in the sunlight. The beast spun and ran off, massive legs driving him across the desert; he quickly disappeared from view.

"Think we'll ever see him again?" asked Keja.

"Not for a while," Giles answered. Whether Red Mane returned or not, they had done what they could to get closer to the city.

They did not expect to see anything of him or the other beasts for several more days and were shocked when a shaggy creature cautiously entered camp in mid-afternoon. It said nothing but seated itself to one side and waited and watched, tiny eyes darting to and fro.

As the day wore on, other beasts arrived. At nightfall Petia and Keja prepared a large kettle of barley soup flavored with spindly herbs Petia had found nearby. They took it to the beasts and set it before them.

"None of them has spoken a word to us," Keja said. His uneasiness had grown as more and more of the beasts entered their camp. "It's as if they are waiting for our redheaded friend to return."

"They probably are," Petia replied. "He might have warned them not to talk with us. Cautious, I suppose."

They built a fire against the inky night; soon after, the red-maned one and another beast appeared out of the dark. "That is all of us," he said.

Giles saw how weary Red Mane was. "I didn't expect you to return so soon. We will talk in the morning after you've rested. Eat now and visit with your friends."

The following morning, the travelers and the beasts sat down to a long discussion.

"Shahal," Red Mane said, "was once the jewel of the desert, a vital stopping place on the caravan road. We were well-known to human caravaners. Trade prospered, both human and Shahal benefiting." He let out a low howl of anguish, then shook his head so hard that dust flew in all directions from the thick mop.

"The caravans began to dwindle and eventually disappeared. Finally the Skeleton Lord and his minions came. We thought they were only new and odd humans, but they were the ones choking off trade—trade Shahal needed." Red Mane made a curious gesture, tugging at the back of his mane as he shook his head.

"Let me guess," Petia said. "The Skeleton Lord moved in and tossed you out."

Red Mane nodded sadly. "Since then, we have lived an aimless existence in the desert."

"Why didn't you try to build a new city?" asked Keja. "If you couldn't fight this Skeleton Lord, you could at least found another city."

"We tried, a few times we tried. He destroys all we attempt. We live amid the dunes, scrabbling out a pitiful existence. No caravans, no trade, no Shahal. We are the most pitiful of all creatures." Red Mane finally brought the tale to a halt. "Will you help us to recover our Shahal? There is great wealth there, a fabulous room of treasure gathered during the trade years. We do not want it; we have no use for it. It is yours if you help us to win back the city."

Giles answered with his own question. "Do you know anything about a key belonging to the Skeleton Lord? A gold key that has something to do with the Harifim religion?"

"We do not know of religion. The Harifim are a desert people. We think that the skeleton men come from the Harifim. But it is not their choice."

"So we still don't know if the key is in Shahal," Petia said in exasperation. "We could be following a feral slug."

"A feral slug?" Keja asked. "That sounds disgusting."

"I mean not finding anything at all after a great deal of effort."

"I understand." Keja raised his eyes to the sky. "A feral slug," he muttered as he sat down.

Giles pulled out his map again. "Do you know Makar, or Lis Abem, or Calaret, or Darestra?"

"All were cities on the old caravan track," Red Mane said, squinting. "Darestra was on the coast, the others scattered along the route."

"All on the map," Giles muttered, "but not Shahal. I wonder why? Not just a deserted city, but a lost city, begging your pardon, Red Mane. And the domain of the Skeleton Lord." Giles folded the map and said with finality, "The best place I can think of to look for the key."

"We want the key; they want their city back. We could all be in trouble," Keja said.

"No doubt," Giles said. He reached over and touched Red Mane's arm. "We will help you, and you will help us. Agreed?"

Red Mane nodded and rose to his feet. He faced the other beasts and spoke in his tongue-tangling language. The beasts stood and growled.

Giles tensed, but Petia sensed the true emotional current and laid a calming hand on his arm.

Turning to the humans and Trans, eyes moist, Red Mane said, "They are happy. The caravaners stopped believing in us. It has been a long time. We return to Shahal!"

Giles hoped it was so—and that the fourth key to the Gate of Paradise would be their reward.

Chapter Eight

The beasts distanced themselves from their new allies, too long in the desert to easily consort with others. Red Mane became their spokesman, but even he showed signs of uneasiness around the humans and Trans.

Giles, knowing the Trans woman's ability to touch emotion, spoke to Petia about it. "We don't know a thing about what they are thinking. We know only what Red Mane decides to tell us. I might be too suspicious, but I wonder if the beasts are just using us."

"As we're using them," Petia added.

Giles only nodded.

"Don't you trust them?" she asked.

"I don't distrust them, at least not at the moment. We just don't know enough about them. I believe what Red Mane told us about Shahal and that they once lived there, but how will they react when we get to the city or confront the Skeleton Lord's men? How will they do in a fight? Red Mane certainly didn't show us much bravery. One cut and he surrendered."

"I'll see what I can do," Petia said. "I haven't used it much lately, so I'm out of practice. Maybe I should have been practicing on you and Keja." Her eyes gleamed impishly.

"Don't you dare let me catch you doing that," Giles said. "My thoughts and emotions are private." The old soldier in him valued his snippets of privacy more than anything else; it was in too short a supply under normal circumstances. Giles wanted to be free to feel as his nature dictated.

But it wasn't too much to ask the Trans to spy on Red Mane and the others. Giles counted that as part of their "war" to win the key to Paradise.

"Oh, so now you want me to trust you and Keja. That's

not what you were saying a few weeks back. I remember the very words, 'I still don't trust you two.' You don't trust me, but I'm supposed to trust you. You can't have it both ways, Giles. Remember that."

He heaved a deep sigh as she stalked off. What bothered him the most was that she had cut to the heart of the problem. Traveling with a pair of thieves had done little to instill trust in him, though.

Giles went to muster the ragtag band and get them moving. This, at least, was something he did well and without getting anyone upset.

The company now looked like a troop of soldiers as they followed the Track of Fourteen. The humans and Trans walked most of the time, leading their *lirjan*. The beasts ambled along behind. At times Red Mane joined Giles and the others, but mostly he stayed with the other beasts, chattering away in their incomprehensible tongue.

The sun beat down fiercely on the Track as it stretched across the desert, and occasionally they were beset by sandstorms. Sudden winds filled the air with stinging particles, which obscured the Track and forced the company to halt and wait for the wind to die before moving on. And through the heat and dust and wind they continued on, knowing that the elements were the least part of their ordeal—Shahal and the Skeleton Lord lay ahead.

"I don't understand this land," Keja mumbled. "Not a cloud in the sky, the sun blazing down. Then the wind comes up, blows everything into obscurity, and goes away just as quickly. It's not a land to live in."

"The gods created the desert for themselves, Anji told us," Giles replied. "Red Mane calls it the garden of the gods."

"They can have it. Once we find that key, we leave."

"There's no reason for staying then," Giles agreed.

The heat and constant scorching from the sun sapped the foursome's strength. They required more water than the beasts, and the goatskin became dangerously lean. When they stopped for the evening, Giles brought the matter up to Red Mane.

"Water is running low. We don't know where to find it, but you or one of the other beasts must know. You need water, too, don't you?"

"We know where to find water." Red Mane frowned and tugged at his knotted hair as if he had never considered such a request. Finally, as if coming to a momentous conclusion, he said, "There is a spot, a pleasant place. There are trees and plants. The animals come to drink where the water bubbles up from beneath the ground and makes a small lake."

"An oasis," Giles said. "Could you find it and fill the waterskins for us? Keja and Petia and the boy are losing their strength, and I'm in none too good condition."

Red Mane looked at Giles. "Yes. Water is important in the desert. There is some danger, but I will have someone go. They will be careful."

"How dangerous?"

"Only a little. Usually the animals share grudgingly. We all depend on the same water. Still, it is good to be careful, especially if the Skeleton Lord stirs."

Giles didn't even want to consider that possibility. Did the Skeleton Lord know they were coming? To regain Shahal? To take away the key?

The party chosen by Red Mane returned two days to great "celebration." Giles watched uneasily as the beasts clawed and tore at one another, growling and gnashing teeth. In spite of this wildness, everyone in the party was careful not to waste any of the hard-won, precious water.

"They do carry on, don't they?" said Keja, his uneasiness outpacing Giles'. The small thief's hand never strayed far from his sword hilt.

"They delivered the water we needed. Apparently, they don't require anywhere near as much as we do. We're going to have to ration."

"No more cat baths," Keja said loud enough for Petia to overhear. The Trans woman sniffed and turned away, pointedly ignoring him.

Giles started to reprimand Keja; keeping peace in the party proved difficult enough without adding new twigs to the fires of animosity and distrust. Still, he didn't think Keja meant the words. This was his way of joking. It fell flat, but he intended no harm. If anything, Giles saw

something more between Keja and Petia—and they would
be the last ones to admit it.

The party continued along the Track of Fourteen. Each
evening Giles pulled out the map and attempted to determine their location. Some evenings he smiled confidently as
he put the map away. Other times he finished with a scowl.
They were approaching an area marked as the Calabrashio
Seas. This worried Giles; they trod across bone-dry desert.

One evening, as Giles finished studying the map, Red
Mane asked, "May I show this wonder to my friends?"
Without comment, Giles handed over the map. He
watched, amused at the beasts' joking comments about the
portraits of their friends on the map. Giles retrieved the
map and looked at the illuminations more carefully, then
frowned. If he didn't know this map was centuries old, he'd
think the artist had used Red Mane and several others in
the band as subjects.

When they reached the Calabrashio Seas, Giles could do
no more than stare numbly.

"I've never seen anything like this," Petia muttered.

"I've never even *heard* of anything like it," said Keja. He
lifted the bone glare protection so that it rested on the top
of his head. He wiped sand and sweat away, then spat. "We
can't cross *that*."

Giles almost agreed with him. The sand seas undulated
with the motions of enormous waves in constant motion. It
was as if they stood on an ocean strand watching the endless
incoming tide.

Under the lapping waves of gritty brown sand, the Track
of Fourteen disappeared without a trace. No matter how
they strained their eyes, there was no evidence of an end to
the Calabrashio nor a road continuing onward.

They drew back, irrationally fearful the lapping waves
would rush forward and swallow them.

"Let's get out of sight," said Petia. "Of the waves.
They . . . they make me seasick."

"Yes, let's humor her," spoke up Keja, but he obviously
shared her affliction.

Giles nodded. "This is marked on the map but not as
sand. I anticipated something, but I didn't expect this." His

face had lost some of its color, even under his sun-tanned, leathery skin.

"We can make our way around it," Petia said. "Surely there is an edge to it. What does the map show?"

"We camp," Giles said forcefully. "I want to ask Red Mane why he didn't warn us of this."

When Giles did talk with Red Mane, he was not encouraged. "I'm sorry," the beast said. "We thought you knew. The sand seas are huge, no way around them unless you spend many dangerous, waterless weeks. The seas stretch across to the Cliffs of Agrib, where the waves of sand break upon the cliffs. It is dangerous there. We would be buried immediately."

The idea that Red Mane considered the end of their journey more dangerous than what Giles saw now tested his determination to pursue the fourth key to the Gate of Paradise. But retreating hardly seemed preferable to continuing on. He knew the hardship behind. Perhaps it wasn't so dangerous in front.

"How can we get through, Red Mane?" Giles stared blankly at the map before him.

"It is dangerous and one must be careful, but it has been done. In the old days, even the caravans crossed it."

"How? The sand shifts all the time, sliding up and down in waves and troughs."

Red Mane stared down toward the shifting mass, as if he could see through the dark. "There are places where it is bare and not all one sea of sand. There are many seas. Sometimes you can find your way between seas." He looked at Giles. "It is the only way across."

"You know the way, then?" Giles asked, encouraged.

"No. When we beasts were driven out of Shahal, we were harried by the skeleton warriors, herded into the seas. Those of us you see survived. We wandered for days in the seas. Some of us were separated and we never saw them again."

Giles rummaged in his pack for the compass the dhouti had given him. In the firelight he studied compass and map, wondering if he could—if he should—lead this small company through the treacherous terrain ahead. Did he want to be responsible for their safety, for their very lives?

"I guess there's no choice," Giles said, his mind made up. "We've got to wade through the Calabrashio. Once into it, we'll have to keep going, no stopping. We may find places to rest, but not to sleep. It must be thirty miles wide. We'll start in the morning."

The sand shifted beneath the travelers' feet, and dust blew off the top of the waves, as spray does from ocean waves. The company found it impossible to keep the sifting sand from their mouths and noses, no matter how tightly they tied cloth over them. Even through the thin slits in the glare goggles, fine dust seeped, more like water than sand.

Sand sifted into their boots and found its way into the cracks and crevices of their clothing. Water became even more precious now, and they drank only a little at midday. Even the beasts suffered severe dehydration, the water they did allow themselves causing stomach cramps.

The sand ebbed and flowed before them. Giles kept his compass handy, protected from the sand. During lulls in the wind's savage assault, he would pull it out quickly and try to focus on some landmark ahead.

But no true reference points existed. Sand dunes thirty yards ahead would disappear without a trace, sinking down into the brown, heat-soaked death of the sand sea. If he tried to follow such ghosts, they veered off course.

Giles tried to keep his eyes straight ahead on the compass setting. He began counting steps, even though this served little purpose. The others staggered behind him, beasts, Trans and human, trying to maintain a straight line and ignore the ever-changing terrain.

Even Anji, who was more accustomed to the heat than the other humans, suffered from the lack of water and sleep. He rubbed his eyes frequently, faltered more and more often, but never complained. Petia looked imploringly at Giles, but the bone goggles hid any hint of sympathy. She finally got a piece of rope from Keja, looped one end around Anji's waist and tied the other to her belt. This way, if Anji stumbled and fell, she would know.

Occasionally they found a clear and quiet place to rest briefly. No speech was possible; their mouths had turned to sand and their throats closed. Giles would wait until the restless sand rolled toward them again, then he'd urge the group to their feet and onward. Hunger attacked them, but there was no place to prepare a meal. Thirst was a constant companion. Worst of all, they began to drift alone, each lost in a closed prison of his or her own mind.

At sunset the wind died slightly and the sand shifted less as if the tide had begun to ebb.

By the end of the first day, most staggered rather than walked. Giles urged them on into the night. To stop was to die. When the sun went down, the Calabrashio turned freezing.

"How can it be so hot during the day and turn cold so quickly at night?" Keja asked.

Giles pointed above. Thousands of stars littered the heartless black sky. "No cloud cover; nothing to hold the heat in. It dissipates rapidly from sand."

They paused, retied packs on their *lirjan* and wondered if even these hardy animals might survive. After their all too brief rest, the sands began to move again. Giles found a constellation on which to concentrate and followed it, plodding on through the night.

When the first light came, Giles pulled out his compass to check. Petia saw him clasping his forehead.

"What's wrong, Giles?" she asked.

"I forgot that the sky turns during the night. I followed that cluster of stars and we've curved south. What a fool!"

"Don't be so hard on yourself," Petia said. "We're all tired and dazed. You, too."

"But I ought to know better."

"How far are we off course?"

"The gods only know. We may have made some progress east, but probably an equal distance south. When we do get through the Calabrashio, we'll be well south of the Track."

"Can't we change now to correct our course?" Petia asked.

"I can try." Giles sighed. "Don't tell the others. We have problems enough without them knowing that I've blundered so."

Petia nodded. Doubt was dangerous and dissension now

would kill them. She put her hand on Giles' arm in understanding and encouragement. "We'll make it," she said.

He shook his head and grimaced, but gratitude shone in his eyes.

While they walked, Giles berated himself for the error of the night before. Finally he realized that what was done was done. He convinced himself that he wasn't made of iron and that he alone of the party wasn't indestructible and infallible. Even worse, Giles came to the conclusion that, while he had experience in such forced marches from the twenty years spent during the Trans War, this meant nothing compared to the fact he had aged.

"Old man, keep moving," he said to himself. The words barely left his gummy mouth, but they had their effect. So what if he had grown old? He wasn't ready for the grave yet—and the Gate to Paradise beckoned.

If Giles pushed himself, he demanded no less of the others. Whenever their determination flagged, he drove and harried until they were moving again. He took advantage of every lull in the undulating sand; he knew it was the only way to achieve victory over the Calabrashio.

Keja grumbled that they needed a rest.

"We can't afford to, Keja. We could be lost in here forever if we don't keep moving."

"I don't think a rest would hurt," Keja responded. "I can hardly put one foot after the other. Don't let being leader go to your head."

"I never asked for the position," Giles replied. He held the compass for Keja. "Here. You lead for a while. I'll be happy to follow, as long as you stay headed east."

Keja turned away, spat and walked off.

"What was that about?" Petia asked.

"I'm not sure," Giles said. "Keja's unhappy because I'm leading, but it might be more than that. Try to find out what's bothering him."

After the next short rest, Keja placed himself at the back of the beasts, dissociating himself from Giles, Petia and Anji. Giles knew the signs of mutiny brewing, but he didn't know the reason.

The long, hot afternoon wore into evening, then the

sudden darkening into night. Giles, staggering drunkenly, again made the rounds, encouraging everyone—except Keja, who remained distant. During the rest, Giles looked at the map and made calculations. If the map were accurate, they should be near the eastern edge of the sand seas by morning—and Giles dared not tell the party. He feared that the map might not be accurate or his calculations wrong. Such disappointment might be the end of their fragile alliance.

When morning came and they still staggered through the waves of sand, Giles nearly despaired. It was all Giles could do to force himself to his feet and urge the others on.

They had been walking for only an hour after the morning rest when Anji cried out. "The edge!"

Ahead of them lay the flat plain, looking almost the same as it had three days earlier when they found the Calabrashio Sea blocking their way. The mid-morning heat shimmered off its surface, but to the party, weary of waves and troughs of sand, the unmoving surface looked like an oasis. Boulders and sandstone columns offered shade.

They staggered forward, stumbling like sailors newly ashore when they reached the solid, unshifting ground. The beasts broke into a lope, heading for the nearest available shade. The humans and Trans shuffled after them with only enough energy to move one foot in front of the other.

Upon reaching the shade, they dropped, exhausted. Red Mane came to take the waterskin and share out water. Giles had only enough energy to pour some water for the *lirjan* and caution Red Mane that the water was still rationed.

But Giles exulted. They had conquered the treacherous Calabrashio. He lay back and closed his eyes.

Once he had seen that everyone had water, Red Mane collapsed with his back against the stone. No one moved for a long time. When the sun moved around to glare into Giles' face, he roused himself from his exhausted stupor. He stood and Petia opened one eye to look at him.

"What are you doing?" she asked.

"We've got to eat. We haven't had a decent meal in three days. We must have carried the supplies for some reason."

Before Giles got the meal started, the beasts cried out in agitation. He looked toward the boulder where they were still huddled in the shade. "I wonder what that's about?" he said to Petia.

Then he heard Red Mane shout, "Djinn, djinn!"

Giles saw a swirling dust devil moving across the plain. "Quick, find shelter," he yelled to Petia. But she was already running toward Anji, shouting as she went.

His mind snapping from its fatigue-induced lethargy, Giles immediately saw the danger. The man ran after Petia, shouting, "Wait, come back!"

The dust devil swerved, aiming itself for the woman and boy. Giles stopped, watching in mute horror as it surrounded them, obscuring them from his sight.

The dust cleared for a few seconds, and he saw Petia grab the boy. Almost instantly the swirling wind caught her and hurled her to the ground. Giles stumbled toward them. The wind stopped lateral movement, intent on playing with the two Trans caught in the vortex.

Giles plunged into the whirling brown mass. One groping hand found a leg, grabbed and hung on. From the size, he knew it was Anji. He pulled the boy close to him and staggered out of the small tornado. He set the boy down and shouted in his ear. "Run. Run to the boulders and hang on to Keja."

Intending to now rescue Petia, Giles spun around. Of the Trans woman, he saw nothing. The thick wall of whirling dust had become impenetrable, the sand able to strip the flesh from his bones.

Giles heard a cry. Petia? Then nothing. He stood facing the deadly column of sand, torn between suicide and facing the knowledge he had not tried to save Petia. Or her lifeless body.

Chapter Nine

Giles stared, caught up in the agony of indecision. To plunge into that maelstrom of cutting sand meant his death, too, but to leave Petia? He didn't think she had survived, but she might have.

The indecision vanished when he heard the djinn's mocking laugh. Without hesitation, Giles fought his way into the leaping, cutting pillar of dust, searching for Petia. His lips thinned to a line; he dared not let the sand fill his mouth and choke him. Blindly, he flailed about seeking her. The flesh dissolved from his hands, his face. Red agony burned in his veins now. The bone goggles he wore blinded him in the darkness of the djinn's mischief and did little to hold back the dust.

He fought against the buffeting winds—and he found her. Giles almost fell over the writhing woman but managed to keep his balance. He grabbed Petia's shoulders and assisted her to her feet. When she was standing, he put one arm around her waist and drew his sword, awkwardly thumbing the inscription and feeling the blaze of energy. The enemy might be only a mass of swirling dust, but Giles' anger knew no bounds. If the power of the sword allowed them to fight their way out, he'd use it!

Barely had he leveled the sword when a corridor through the shroud of brown opened before them. Giles held the sword before him and half carried Petia to the perimeter of the dust storm. As they cleared the edge of the whirlwind and stumbled into the hot desert sun, Giles swung his blade mightily at the axis of the vortex. He knew that it was an empty gesture, but his anger at the djinn knew no limits.

Giles heard a howl from the miniature tornado's core. The whirling dust stilled and fell to the desert floor, revealing an immense djinn in human guise who made an obscene gesture and disappeared.

Sheathing the sword, Giles assisted Petia, lowering her to the ground to examine the scratches she had suffered.

"You're not so bad off," he said. "No, don't try to talk." He gently wiped away a gooey mixture of spittle and sand from her lips. "You rest now." She tried to speak again, but he silenced her, knowing what she tried to ask. "Anji is fine. Now you rest."

This time, she did relax. Whether she slept or not, Giles didn't know, but she was safe. That was all that mattered.

Keja dropped down beside Giles, face strained. "The djinn is gone. I tried to reach you but the dust . . ."

"We'll be all right," Giles said. Whether Keja had tried to reach him was a moot point. He laughed, somewhat harshly. "We survive a sea of moving sand and yet a prankster spirit almost kills us."

"I'll stand guard," Keja declared, hand on sword.

"Do as you wish. I just want to rest." Giles curled up in a shady spot, not noticing the hard rocks beneath him. As tired as he was, he might have been lying on a bed of flower petals. He came groggily awake when he heard Anji cry out.

"We're trapped inside a bottle," the boy shouted.

Giles wiped his eyes again and looked around. Most of the beasts still slept. He gazed about him, unbelieving. Shards of light splintered against a translucent surface and reflected painfully bright rays into his eyes.

A glass wall encircled them. Giles strode across the enclosure and reached out to assure himself that this was not some fatigue-induced nightmare. The hot glass caused him to jerk his hand away—the glass prison wall was all too real.

The others had roused and came to Giles' side with a barrage of questions. No matter what happened, Giles thought, they looked to him for answers. Like it or not, he was the leader.

"I don't know what happened," he said. "Anji discovered it. The djinn, probably. Angry at being driven off."

Red Mane shook his head. "Not the djinn. The Skeleton Lord."

"How do we get out of this one, Giles?" Keja asked, standing back and looking upward.

In the marketplace the rough glass would be called poor, but it imprisoned them effectively and grew increasingly hotter by the minute. Giles wrapped his hand in a fold of his robe and tapped on the thick surface. It wouldn't break easily.

The beasts gibbered nervously among themselves. Red Mane tried to still them, but their panic grew. "It will bring us death," one of them said. Giles' anger rose at being penned like this, and he called to Red Mane.

"Can you see through? Is there anyone outside?"

Red Mane walked around the circle of glass, stopping to peer. "I can't see anyone out there. If the Skeleton Lord did it, he wouldn't leave anyone on guard. He knows that we can't escape."

"Don't give up so easily," Giles snapped. He tried to force calmness on himself and his thoughts, but it wasn't easy. In all his years of soldiering, nothing like this had ever happened to him. Facing a sword was one thing, magic another.

Giles knelt where the glass met the desert. He took his dagger and dug into the soil. "Perhaps we can dig under the glass."

Willing hands came to his assistance. As he loosened the hard-packed desert soil, others scooped it away. His blade dug deeper and deeper, but always it met the glass wall; the bottle plunged deep into the earth. The perspiration rolled off Giles' forehead, stinging his eyes. Dig as he might, he couldn't reach the bottom of the glass. At last he sat back, looked at his helpers and shook his head.

"It's no good," he said. "I don't think we'll ever dig under it."

The beasts moaned. "Die here," one said.

"No, we won't die here. We *will* get out." Giles detested this self-pity and wondered if recruiting the beasts had been such a good idea. Give him a small squad of determined volunteers over recruits any day.

Keja moved to the center of the bottle, looking upward. He could see the top of the glass enclosure yawning open, like a candle chimney. Because of the sun's glare, the small thief couldn't estimate its height. Slowly he unwound the rope around his waist.

He found his triple hook and attached it to the end of the rope. "Everyone stand to one side. I'll see if I can hook the top."

He swung the hook in an ever-widening arc, dipping it low to the ground and then up into the air. The hook swung up, but struck the glass about twenty feet above their heads and tumbled back down.

"Wrong approach," Keja muttered. He coiled the rope carefully at his feet. This time he swung the hook faster and faster in a vertical circle. When he had the hook traveling at a good speed, he released it upward.

The hook flew true, arching from the center of the circle and reaching for the top of the glass wall. The rope played out of its circle, reached its end, and continued to fly upward. But once again the hook did not reach the top of the glass enclosure.

He tried over and over, but each time the hook fell back, once nearly hitting a beast. Finally, arm-weary and frustrated, Keja gave up.

"What now?" he said to Giles.

"Let me try my sword. It worked getting clear of the djinn's dust devil." He widened his stance and pulled the weapon from its scabbard. "Stand back everyone. We don't need anyone hit by splintering glass."

Giles selected a spot on the glass wall, thumbed the inscription and felt the sword's energy in his hand and arm. He placed the sword point against the glass and pushed. Nothing. He stepped back a step and swung a weak blow. A tingle rushed up his arm, but the glass held.

He took the sword with two hands and swung with all his might. Energy flowed from the sword and the glass shimmered through pretty rainbows but did not break.

"I don't think that's going to do it," he said, examining the spot he'd struck and noting he hadn't even scratched the glass.

Anji let out a wordless cry of amazement. Giles squinted through the glass and saw the outline of a beast outside their enclosure, trying to peer in.

"I forgot about her," Red Mane cried. "I exiled her for two days for defecating in my presence. She must have finally caught up with us."

"Shout to her," Petia said. "If we can talk, I have an idea."

Red Mane stood nose to nose with the beast outside the glass and bellowed in his strange tongue.

The beast outside made movements with her mouth, but those inside heard nothing.

Red Mane walked to the center of the circle and bellowed again. Then he cupped his ear and listened. The others held their breath, not wishing to interfere. No sound came back. Red Mane's voice disappeared into the bright blue sky.

"She cannot hear us," Red Mane said.

"Petia, can you communicate with her?" Giles asked. "With your mind?"

"I can try." Petia sat opposite the beast, seeing only distorted images through the glass. She gathered herself, concentrating. Giles had told her to practice, to learn to tap the beasts' emotions. Her success thus far had been limited. Now their lives depended on her feeble Trans ability. The perspiration dripped from her forehead, but she ignored it. If she failed, they would all bake to death inside the glass.

She opened her mind, concentrating on the simple, emotion-laden message she wished to send.

Beast, free us! With this went her fears, her hopes, her overpowering need to insure Anji's safety.

The beast outside became agitated, looking up to the sky and then out into the desert. Petia experienced the panic as if it were her own. Vague pictures formed, confusing ones. She tried to sort them out to use them.

Sleek, Petia sent, knowing the beast's name, at least within her own mind. *Fire!*

Petia shook with the exertion. So much effort for such small information. And Petia didn't even know if this simple plan might work, if Sleek would understand.

The female beast hesitantly piled dried branches against one side of the bottle. Her movements, the way her shadow bobbed across the translucence of the bottle-prison, showed her confusion. But she obeyed the emotionally charged commands Petia arrowed in her direction.

"Sit quietly," Petia cautioned the others in the prison. "The storm of emotion confuses me, and I might need to reach her again."

"What's happening?" demanded Keja. Giles silenced him with a curt gesture. Keja fell into a sullen silence.

Sitting quietly by the glass, Petia closed her eyes. She tried to follow Sleek's movements, occasionally encouraging her with mind-murmuring *yes!* and *good!* Petia tried to remain relaxed when she sniffed—when Sleek sniffed! —the first curl of smoke.

The brush outside burst into flame, visible through their glass confinement. Giles had to motion Keja to silence; he saw Petia's difficulty in keeping contact with the beast outside.

Petia urged Sleek to pile on more brush, to keep adding to the fire until it was so hot that she could not come near enough to throw more wood on. Finally, Petia received a blast of outright fear of the flames from the beast.

Petia collapsed in a limp heap. "There's nothing to do until the fire burns down. Let's hope that the heat crystallizes the glass enough for your sword to do its work."

They sat in silence, watching the flames leaping outside the glass. When the piled brush became ashes, Petia motioned to Giles. He pulled his sword again and approached the glass. Weak as he was from the heat, he walked with firm stride and confidence.

Petia's eyes glowed when she lightly brushed across his emotions. Giles put on no act; he radiated confidence and this buoyed her own sagging spirits.

Giles thumbed the sword's inscription and placed its tip against the glass. It quivered and hummed, then broke through. A small triangular piece of glass fell to the sand. A second blow caused larger pieces to break off. Within a few minutes he had enlarged the opening enough for all to crawl through.

Petia was the first one out. She dashed to Sleek. Petia threw her arms around the beast and cried, "Sleek, you were wonderful!"

The others poured out of the glass enclosure into the midday sun. By comparison with their bottlelike imprisonment, the desert seemed cool.

"Keja, see to the water. Everyone must be nearly dehydrated. Careful with it, but a double ration for everyone."

When everyone had drunk their fill, found shade wherever they could and regained some measure of strength, Giles called Red Mane, Keja and the Trans together. "We can't stay on the Track any longer. The djinn were bad enough. If Red Mane is correct, the Skeleton Lord knows about us—and wants us dead. We must be careful from now on and anticipate another attack or we might not be so lucky."

It took a good deal of urging to get the group moving after their ordeal. They understood but were weary and thirsty and not inclined to go on. It took Giles some time to convince Red Mane that his only hope of regaining Shahal was to attack, not to retreat.

Giles wondered if he believed that himself. But it got the beasts back onto the Track. For the key, Giles would do anything—or almost anything. Where would he draw the line?

When they first saw the oasis, shimmering on the horizon, they thought it a mirage. But the beast who had scouted assured Red Mane that it was real. As eager as the party was for water, their strength neared its end. But they could only struggle on until they reached the promised cool, green and wet oasis.

Adrenaline pumped through their veins as they reached the rim dividing desert from oasis and sent them rushing forward to plunge their faces into the pool. Giles ran among them, cautioning them not to drink too much or they would be sick.

"Giles," shouted Petia, "you are like an old woman, a nanny!" She threw water at him. For a moment, Giles bristled, then relaxed and joined in the play. The water felt *good* against his skin.

Anji took a small drink, then led the *lirjan* to one end of the pool. The pack animals drank noisily, but in a moment he pulled them away from the pool and tethered them to a tree nearby.

The boy started back to the pool, then froze, eyes wide. He swallowed, then called out in a voice almost too low to be heard, "Master Giles. A djinn!"

Giles swung around, hand on sword. Anji pointed to the pool. Only a small swirl of bubbles rose from the depths.

"Master Giles, truly I saw a djinn. He came from beneath the water and looked around as if he didn't believe what he was seeing."

"Quiet," Giles ordered. He stood, watching. The bubbles surged to the surface at a quicker rate now.

"The djinn are not usually harmful," Red Mane said, sidling up next to Giles. "I truly believe that the one who swept up Petia and Anji in the dust devil did not know that they would be injured. Their fun is a bit malicious, but they are only playing. Perhaps you can trick this one in return, and he will leave us alone."

"How would we do that?" Giles asked.

"We must lay a trap for him. He is a shy one, to disappear like that," Red Mane answered.

Anji kept his eyes on the pool, hoping to see the djinn again. Keja and Giles sat with him, wondering what they could do to disarm the djinn. Otherwise, they were certain to suffer some indignity from the creature sooner or later.

"I wonder if djinn like wine," Keja mused. "Or maybe ale. What I wouldn't give for a flagon now."

"Yes, wine." The voice ebbed across the water from the center of the pool.

"Do we have a djinn who talks?" Giles asked.

"You were speaking of wine?" The djinn rose from the water, torso visible. His arms were folded across his chest and muscles in his brown shoulders rippled.

"Good evening," Giles said, more calmly than he felt.

"Good evening. You mentioned wine? A good one, I trust, of fine vintage—and not too dry. I loathe dry wines. Comes from being in the desert for so long, I suppose."

"Yes. A splendid drink, is it not?" Giles agreed, relaxing somewhat. It was difficult to feel menaced by this creature who prattled on at such lengths. "Warms the stomach and is good for the constitution."

"You have some, then?" the djinn asked.

Forever after, Giles would not know what prompted him. "Yes, we do. Would you like some?"

No answer came. The djinn seemed to dissolve. The next moment it appeared, dry, in front of Giles.

"Where is it?" the djinn asked eagerly.

"Wait," Giles said. "Just a minute now. We can't afford

to let you have the entire wineskin." He motioned to Keja behind his back. "You seem anxious. We can't let you drink it all. And we expect something in exchange. Wine is not easy to obtain out here in the desert. You, of all, uh, people, must realize that."

"Oh, it's been so long since I've had a drink of wine," the djinn moaned.

Keja turned and walked away. "Careful with that skin now, Keja," Giles called after him. "There's only a little left."

"Where? Where is it?" the djinn cried.

"In a moment. What do we get in return?"

"Anything, what would you like?"

"I don't know what you can give us," Giles said. "Food, perhaps. Directions to Shahal. Something to protect us from the sun. I don't know. You tell me."

"Yes, yes," the djinn replied anxiously. "All those. Now the wine, please."

"It's over this way. Follow me. There's a slit in the skin, though. You must be careful. You'll have to crawl in. That should be no problem."

The djinn drew himself up, disappeared into a vaporous puff, then appeared again. "Of course not."

The goatskin lay flat on its side. Keja had emptied the last of the water from it.

"Just crawl in there," Giles said. "But you be sure to leave some for the rest of us."

The djinn disappeared again. All that could be seen was a slight puffing of the goatskin.

"Quick, the stopper," Giles whispered.

Keja thrust the stopper into the mouth of the goatskin.

"There's no wine in here." The anguished cry was muffled by the goatskin.

Giles knelt by the skin. "What a shame. I seem to have made a mistake in hinting some might be found there," he answered.

"You will suffer for the indignity you heap upon me!" shouted the djinn. "I promise eternal vengeance!"

"We've had enough of djinn's tricks. We don't want any more. We've captured you."

"You can't do that. I haven't harmed you. I never wanted

to be a djinn. The Skeleton Lord did this to me as punishment. I'm really a man."

"We don't believe you," Giles said. "Djinn tell lies, too."

Petia came to kneel by Giles and Keja. "What are you going to do?" she whispered.

"Worry him a bit, then strike a bargain." He held his finger to his lips while the djinn continued to plead. Grinning at having turned the tables on a djinn, they listened as the creature alternately begged and threatened.

"Please let me out," the djinn pleaded. "I was a caravaner once, a scout and a guard. I know this area well. I can help you on your travels. Is there anyone out there? Oh, no, don't abandon me here forever! Not in a smelly *goatskin*! How degrading!"

Giles spoke up as if he had been away. "Are you still shouting in there, djinn? I thought you might be asleep by now. We were getting ready to bed down for the night."

"Please. Please let me out. It's stuffy in here—awful. I will help you, I promise. I really am a human. I was cruelly turned into a djinn by the evil Skeleton Lord."

"We can't keep him in there forever, Giles," Keja whispered. "We need the goatskin. It's the best water bag we have."

"I know," Giles said. "I just want to scare him a little. Maybe he'll be useful to us. If not . . ." He shrugged.

"How did you get changed into a djinn?" Giles asked, lifting his voice so the trapped djinn could hear.

"I told you. The Skeleton Lord. He turned me into one. He used a spell from a big book."

"A likely story," Giles said, beginning to enjoy this. He couldn't forget a djinn—maybe this one—had threatened Anji and Petia with the whirlwind. "I think we're going to leave you inside the goatskin."

"Wait!" the djinn cried. "Wait, please, I beg you."

"Beg me to do what?" Giles goaded.

"I . . . I have many powers, having once been human and now trapped in this djinn form." The goatskin rippled with agitation. Giles shoved the toe of his boot into the side and watched the side jerk back. "I hate the Skeleton Lord for what he's done to me. And you must, also. You must!"

"Why?"

"He imprisoned you in the glass bottle. I saw!"

Giles said nothing. The djinn had witnessed their imprisonment but had done nothing to free them. He didn't feel overly inclined to aid the creature now.

"Together," the djinn cried, "together we can defeat the Skeleton Lord. He is not invincible."

"And you are?"

"Together we can defeat him. I know it. You . . . you can help me return to human form. And I can help you find something worth more than gold!"

"Water is more precious than gold in the desert," said Giles. "We have the water we need. What is it you're referring to?"

"A key. The Skeleton Lord has a special key!"

Keja started to shout out in joy but Giles restrained him. Hardly able to contain his own excitement, he kept his voice calm when he said, "A key? We have no need of a key, but perhaps we can strike a deal. You sound contrite."

"I am!"

Giles motioned for Keja to uncork the goatskin. A wisp of smoke gushed out, then hardened and rose into a column. And the column didn't stop growing until the powerfully muscled djinn loomed a full twenty feet over their heads.

With a single twitch of his massive hand, the djinn could kill all in the camp. He reached down for Giles.

Chapter Ten

Giles Grimsmate's sword whirred as it slid from his sheath—but the movement came far too late. The djinn's immense hand scooped up Giles and held the man dangling and kicking helplessly a dozen feet above the ground.

"Stop him!" Giles heard Petia shriek. From Red Mane came a frightened growl. Of Keja, Giles saw and heard nothing. And he had no time to wonder about the small thief. Giles stared directly into an unwinking, dinner-plate-huge bloodshot eye. Arms trapped at his sides by vaporous fingers turned iron-hard, Giles felt the life fleeing his body. Every breath was harder to suck in than the last.

As he began to pass out, he heard the djinn's plaintive voice. "Are you all right?"

Giles couldn't answer, but faintly, as if from a great distance, he heard the sounds of a sword hacking at flesh.

As suddenly as the djinn had picked him up, the creature released him. Giles fell heavily to the ground, shaken and not sure what had happened. When his eyes focused he saw Keja clinging to the side of the giant djinn, slashing away with his sword.

"Stop him, please, oh please stop him. That *hurts!*"

"Keja," Giles croaked out. "Get away."

The small thief obeyed warily. They all expected further mischief from the oversized djinn.

"I was overcome with joy at being released. I meant only to thank you," the djinn said with hurt dignity. "I did nothing to inspire such attack." The djinn smoothed away wrinkles in the magical substance of his body and began to shrink until he was hardly taller than Giles.

Petia shook her head. Keja glowered. They didn't know whether this djinn would be peaceable or keep his word, if given.

"What is your name?" Petia asked. "It's difficult to talk to you when we don't know your name."

The djinn hung his head. "I'd rather you didn't use it. I have shamed myself before you, and for that I must do penance. If you must address me, just call me Djinn. When I have my own body back, then I'll give voice to my name."

Petia nodded with understanding. Her Trans talent tapped into the djinn's flow of emotions, which almost staggered her with contriteness.

"Have you lived here long?" she asked.

"What is time to a discorporated soul? I don't even know how long ago it was that the Skeleton Lord placed this curse upon me." Giles thought the djinn held back misty tears only through extreme effort. "The other djinn don't play with me—they go and do their pranks by themselves. Even among other djinn, I am an outcast."

"What do you do?"

"I sit, I watch the strange happenings in the desert. Little else amuses me."

"What strange occurrences are these?" Petia prompted.

"Like a man who has appeared in the desert. He is white, like the two men with you, lovely lady. He dresses in black and rides an immense black horse. Above him constantly circles a hawk. I went to see him because he is not of the desert and therefore an amusing curiosity for one such as myself who grows bored with this disembodied existence. I never found out what he seeks." Djinn crossed arms only less muscular than his larger form as he went on. "And the desert tribesmen move west, about a day's journey north of here. I don't think they will visit this oasis. There is another closer to their path."

Keja turned to Giles and asked, "This man in black who Djinn saw. Could he be the same man we encountered in Dimly New?"

Giles frowned and did not answer.

"I see there are beasts with you. I leave them alone. Smelly, awful creatures, though I must admit that this form does not permit me the sense of smell. Damn you, Lord! Why did you have to rob me of my own body?"

The beasts slowly gathered around, staring at Djinn. Giles guessed this was their first opportunity to see one of the spirits without also being on the receiving end of a prank.

"This one will help us regain our home?" Red Mane asked. The skepticism in his voice radiated for all to hear. The beasts began muttering among themselves.

"Shahal?" Djinn asked. "I know the place. Used to trade there until the Skeleton Lord . . ." Djinn's voice trailed off. "If it is your will—and if I can regain my body—I'll help you into Shahal."

"A fair enough trade," Giles said. Keeping his voice level, he added, as if making a last-minute comment. "That key you mentioned. Perhaps it would look nice around the lady's neck." Giles indicated Petia.

"Yes, a token of esteem!" Djinn cried.

"Such a fine token," muttered Keja.

Giles drowned out Keja's snide retort and continued to delve into Djinn's story, intent on finding out as much as possible about the surrounding countryside, the Skeleton Lord, Shahal, and what they could expect when they arrived there.

"Are there other humans who were changed into djinn?" he asked.

"I doubt it. I think the Skeleton Lord did it on a whim, just to see if the spell worked. I've met other djinn in the desert, but they were real djinn and always had been."

Red Mane summoned up enough courage to ask about the desert traveler in black. "What do you know of him?" Giles and the others listened with interest.

"Nothing, really," Djinn replied. "He looked fearsome. I followed him for a while, but I didn't materialize to him. He wasn't traveling fast; he seemed to be searching for something—or someone."

"Giles," Red Mane said slowly, "I think I will send one of my people out to see if he is still in the area. No one rides for pleasure in this desert. He might be a minion of the Skeleton Lord."

Giles agreed that it would be a good idea to find this mysterious stranger but ventured no opinion on the man's allegiance. He doubted the Skeleton Lord and this man in black shared similar goals—or if they did, they each wanted the reward for himself. But what was the reward?

The key to the Gate of Paradise? Giles decided to ponder this at greater length later.

Red Mane withdrew into his own thoughts, trying to determine who would be the best of the beasts for the job. He went to chat with a younger beast, Torn Ear. The youngster nodded, rose and disappeared into the night.

Returning to his place by the fire, Red Mane said simply, "It is done."

Giles asked Djinn to tell them more.

"When the Skeleton Lord came to power in Shahal, he drove out the beasts." Djinn looked at Red Mane. "They hounded you out of the city like beaten curs, is that not right?" The beast silently agreed with this shameful appraisal.

"I was the scout for the next caravan to call at Shahal. We didn't know the Skeleton Lord had taken over. His soldiers surprised the caravan and captured us. For a time we were kept together, but gradually one after another of us disappeared. I'm not sure what happened to them. Possibly other experiments. They weren't very friendly toward me, anyway."

"Is this where the skeleton men come from?" Petia asked.

"Yes, I'm certain that they are the Skeleton Lord's most successful experiment. Once he found that he could turn the men into walking skeletons, he concentrated on that. They became his servants, his army, all he needed for his petty conquests. Several more caravans were captured. Then the caravans stopped using that route. The dhouti must have decided that it was no longer safe to take the Track of Fourteen. No one has crossed it for years. I think. Years have so little meaning to me anymore." Djinn gusted a weighty sigh.

"What was his object?" Giles asked. "What is he after?"

"Power. He wants to extend his power across the desert, then to the cities, Kasha in the north and Kuilla in the south. Already he controls the Harifim."

Giles' eyes lighted up. "That explains much. It explains their religion, their belief in the key. And I think it helps to confirm my belief that the key we seek is at Shahal."

"Ah," said the djinn, "the key *is* important to you. I thought so!"

"What sort of force does he have? What can you tell us about his skeleton men?" Giles still distrusted the djinn and warily avoided discussing the key.

"I truly do not know. In the desert it is said that the original skeleton men captured many Harifim and they, in turn, became skeleton men. It continues. So I do not know how many there are. Very many, to be sure, And there may be other humans who were not transformed. I do not know."

"Could we expect any help from those inside?" Keja asked.

Djinn thought on it, as if it had never occurred to him before. "I cannot tell. I haven't been inside for a long time since there is so little for one such as I to do within the walls of Shahal. The Skeleton Lord changed me into a djinn for his own entertainment. It took me a long time to figure out that I could become invisible. I wonder if real djinn come into existence knowing all these things or if they have to be taught? A manual would have been most helpful to me. When I found out how to do the invisibility, I simply left Shahal to live by myself in the desert. A lonely, tiresome existence."

"I can see why," grumbled Keja, "if you have only yourself to listen to."

"The Skeleton Lord could not see me any better than you can."

"So you don't know if the skeleton men are unhappy with their lot?" Giles asked.

"I don't think they have any feelings. I was bitterly unhappy and expect them to be, also. If they have any brain left to think with, that is. Perhaps they do not," Djinn mused. "My own brain became addled for quite some time. Perhaps they no longer think, only obey."

Petia stirred the fire and added wood. No one spoke for a time. Each was wrapped in thoughts about Shahal and its inhabitants.

After a time Djinn sighed. "I think the Lord is quite mad. I think he was mad when he came to Shahal. The silence of the desert has been known to touch men like that, though as a human I rather enjoyed it. Away from the grind of big cities."

To this Giles had nothing to reply.

The next morning Torn Ear appeared, near exhaustion having run a long distance. Red Mane brought him to Giles and the others so he would not have to repeat his story.

"The stranger in black travels with desert tribesmen not of the Harifim. He is not their captive. I tried to approach and spy on them, but they discovered me and chased me."

"What?" Red Mane stormed. "They will come here."

"No," Torn Ear said. "I led them in a different direction. I may not have your immense experience, ancient one, but I am not stupid."

"Don't let your mouth run away with you," Red Mane warned. He turned and showed the youngling his hindquarters. When Red Mane's anger subsided, he asked, "Where did you last see them?"

"They were heading west. I led them that way, toward the oasis at Dorassa. Then I went north into the rocks and doubled back, leaving no trail."

"Well done." Red Mane turned to Giles. "What do we do now?"

Djinn spoke up. "We are between the Track and the tribesmen. I do not think it wise to stay here much longer."

"I suppose you are right. It has been so pleasant here that it is hard to move on." Leaving the tiny pool of water seemed like abandoning an old friend—or security.

"Travel at night," Djinn said. "There is enough light to see by, and I can guide you. It will be safer." Giles looked skeptically at Djinn, but the spirit appeared sincere. Petia shrugged, indicating she received no contrary indications from the djinn, but who could say what a disembodied spirit's emotions were like? Still, Giles had little choice but to risk following Djinn.

They waited until dark, listening to the silence of the desert and wondering where—and what—the black stranger might be. By the time they finally left the oasis, Giles had decided they faced two enemies: the Skeleton Lord and this man in black.

They traveled a score of miles through the night. The days of rest had refreshed them. By morning, however, they felt the effort of the night's travel and sighed with relief when Giles called a halt.

Djinn scouted for a place that would keep them out of the sun for most of the day.

"What are we going to do when we reach Shahal?" Petia asked, when they had settled down. "How are we going to get inside?"

"We can't attack," Keja said. "That's obvious. Maybe there are some unguarded entrances, some of the entrances the beasts have spoken of. No lord guards every entrance, at least not so a clever thief cannot find a way inside."

"Don't be surprised if Shahal is well patrolled," Giles said. "We'll look carefully and scout when we get there. Maybe that will give us some ideas."

The false dawn found them in a valley shaped like a shallow bowl. The sun rose and they shaded their eyes to look across the landscape. Shahal, carved from solid rock centuries before, rose from the plain, immense and silent in the predawn. Giles found himself speechless, not expecting this. He had built an image of a city spread out across the plain. What else had he assumed wrongly?

A tower of rock rose vertically from the desert floor. Many floors were evident from the balconies outlined by the morning light.

"It's huge," Petia sighed. "If it does hold the key, how will we ever locate it?"

"One thing at a time," Giles said. "The first step is to get in."

Red Mane came up to his side. "We had better find some place to hide during the day. We can be seen too easily here in the middle of the plain, and the skeleton men patrol ceaselessly."

"You're right." Giles looked toward the sides of the valley, several miles away. "Do you have any ideas of the best place to conceal ourselves?"

"There is a small cave along that side that would be cool and keep us out of—"

A murmur rose behind them, and Giles turned to see the cause of it.

The beasts pointed down the valley. The sun glinted off two gates at the foot of the rock city. Slowly, they swung open as if these might be the real Gate to Paradise. Giles listened for the expected rumble but heard nothing.

The company watched as a troop of soldiers marched in neat, trim ranks from the dark cavern behind the gates. Old habits died hard; Giles estimated that the contingent numbered one hundred by the number of officers decked with gold rank stripes. Four squads formed and wheeled into the desert with a precision Giles both envied and feared.

"They're well trained," he said. "Too well trained for my taste. Discipline's good, which is bad for us." He glanced at Red Mane. "How far is it to the cave you mentioned? Can we get there before they see us?"

"I think, perhaps, they have already seen us. We had better run for it."

"You lead, we'll follow." Giles felt his heart pace accelerating. Before battle it was always like this. As much as he hated it, he needed it, also. Battle vindicated his existence; he was more than good at it. He survived.

"Hurry," Giles shouted after Red Mane, as the beast loped off. "If you don't want to be caught." Giles waved to Petia and Keja, who had been tying down their packs in preparation for real flight.

He ran to help Anji with the *lirjan.* The sudden activity had frightened the animals.

"Quiet," Anji soothed. "Easy, my lovely ones. It will be all right." He handed one lead rope to Giles and kept the other two himself. "Come, my sweets." He urged the two *lirjan* into motion and gestured with his head for Giles to fall in behind, knowing that the single animal would follow its two companions.

"How you can sweet-talk those smelly creatures, I'll never know." Giles laughed at a sudden thought. When Anji grew older, what would he be like with women? If the boy gentled odorous, bad-tempered *lirjan* this easily, he'd have his way with just about any woman.

Mind turning to more immediate problems, Giles estimated the distance separating them from the troop. His practiced eye claimed three miles. The disciplined troop would make good time. An individual could outrun a troop of soldiers, but Giles had doubts about his own people and the beasts.

He looked ahead toward the side of the valley. Even if they reached it, the soldiers would know where they had gone. And his group was outnumbered. However, they would put up a fight. They had no other choice, since retreating into the desert was out of the question.

"What's happening?" Giles asked Anji.

"Another troop." Anji pointed at the rock city.

A second gate had swung open on the western side of Shahal, and soldiers were marching smartly out of the shadow. They were closer to the valley edge and quick-stepped.

"They'll cut us off," Giles muttered. "We're going to be captured unless we think of something fast."

He watched in dismay as one squad of the original troop separated from the main body, breaking into a trot. The squad outnumbered them two to one.

The beasts cowered together, all confidence gone, as they watched the military precision of the men advancing toward them.

"Run," Giles shouted. "Back the way we came." As treacherous as the desert was, it presented their only hope to avoid capture.

Petia and Keja ran back to where Giles and Anji stood with the *lirjan.*

"Red Mane," Giles shouted again. "Make them understand. We've got to run."

The beast stood, a look of sadness on his face, and shook his head. The beasts had given up; in their minds they had already been captured.

"We've got to leave the *lirjan,* Giles," Keja said. "We'll never get away if we try to take them. They'll be able to spot us from miles off."

"But our supplies," Petia said. "We won't survive in the desert without food and water."

"Keja's right. Use them as a diversion." Giles pointed and Anji went to the animals, patting each one on the nose before turning and kicking it on the rump. The offended *lirjan* ambled off to the southwest, then broke into a trot.

"Now, hurry." Giles loosened the sword in its scabbard, then ran westward. The others followed.

In the end, the escape attempt proved fruitless. The

humans and Trans ran until their lungs strained and every drop of water drained from their bodies. The sun rose higher and the desert shimmered in the heat. The troop pursued them tirelessly.

"Where's that miserable djinn?" gasped out Keja. "He brought the soldiers down on our necks! He did it!"

Giles had no time to debate the point. Keja might have been right. A more immediate problem faced them, though. Skeleton men surrounded them as they lay gasping in the shade of a boulder. Emotionless, white bones impervious to the burning sun, the skeletal warriors pulled the humans to their feet and bound their hands, not even bothering to take their weapons. To Giles, this amounted to humiliation far exceeding any he had ever known. The skeleton troops counted his sword and skill as trivial.

They prodded Giles and the others silently toward Shahal.

"Been nice knowing you," Keja said as they neared the towering, ornately wrought gate into Shahal.

"We're not dead yet," Giles said, but he shared Keja's feelings. Dread filled him as the gates swung open like a brass-toothed mouth to swallow them.

Chapter Eleven

"We should have fought," Keja grumbled.

"They outnumbered us," Petia reasoned, "and they weren't tired from traveling all night. We would have been killed."

"Can skeletons ever get tired?" asked Keja with ill grace. "Bone tired?" He snorted and leaned against a cold stone wall, arms tightly fastened behind him.

Giles didn't blame the man for his attitude. As a leader, he hadn't done too well. They had been herded into Shahal and thrown into these poxy cells, the likes of which Giles had seldom seen. Even during the Trans War, when he'd spent a short stretch as prisoner of war, he had not endured conditions like these. Even worse, the old gaoler hadn't allowed them to keep their weapons, as the skeleton warriors had; he had a fine sense of fear about him and had hung their swords in a neat row along one wall of the dungeon.

Giles looked around to see how the others were. Their arms were tied behind their backs. They lay where they had been pushed, recovering slowly. He got his knees under him, pushing with his head and shoulders. He steadied himself, then staggered to his feet. With his hands behind him, he had difficulty helping the others. He moved among them, encouraging them to their feet. Keja was the last, his face ashen.

They lowered themselves gingerly onto a bench running along one wall. The gaoler muttered to himself in one corner of the room. Wiping his nose with the back of his hand, he rose from his chair at a small table and came toward them.

He bent down and stared at each of them, then cocked his head to the right. Giles realized that he had only one eye, his left. Blinking and muttering, he turned away and opened the door of another cage in the corner opposite that of the beasts. The captives observed that he was hunch-backed. He returned to them, shuffling and digging inside his dirty robe. His hand finally emerged, bringing with it a knife.

"What are you doing, old man?" Giles asked.

"Cage," the old man answered, gesturing with the knife to the other side of the room. "You." He pointed the blade at Giles' chest.

Giles obeyed, the man using the knifepoint to prod him into the cage. He locked the door with a simple shuttle catch, then returned to the others.

One by one he escorted them into the cage. After he had locked the door for the last time, he stood outside and said, "Hands."

"What?" Keja asked.

"Hands." He made a cutting gesture with the knife. Giles understood and backed up to the cage bars. The old man reached through and cut Giles' bindings, then did the same for the others. When he was finished, he shuffled away to resume his seat at the table.

"I don't think he's very bright," Keja said. "One eye, hunchbacked, filthy misshapen pig." He spat.

"He may not be bright, but he's obviously our gaoler," Petia said. "He got us into the cage quickly enough."

"If we're careful and don't anger him, we may be able to talk ourselves back out of the cage."

"You may be right, Keja," Giles said. "But out of the cage isn't out of the dungeon."

"But it's the first step."

"I wonder why we weren't taken to the Skeleton Lord?" Petia mused. "We're probably not important to him, but I'd think he'd be interested in where we've come from and what we were doing in the desert near Shahal."

"Don't be in too big a hurry to meet the Skeleton Lord," Giles advised. "I doubt it will be much fun."

A banging sounded on the dungeon door. The old hunch-back shuffled to unlock it, then stood back, cowering, shielding his good eye with his hand.

A corpulent man, dressed in gray and hugging a fur cloak

about him, advanced into the room. Behind him stood a tall, emaciated man, dressed in maroon velvet robes. His face was shriveled, as if the dryness of the desert had removed all moisture from it. He stepped past the corpulent man, saying, "It's all right, Leaal, they've been caged."

He advanced across the room to stand before the beasts' cage. "What have we here? The beasts have returned." He smirked—and it turned his skeletal face even uglier. "Not content with their freedom in the desert, they've returned to offer allegiance to their lord. How discerning of them to wish to serve the one who will soon be master of the entire continent!"

The beasts cowered to the back of the cage. Red Mane stood nearest the Skeleton Lord. He glanced at the man, but even he did not have enough courage to face him directly.

The Skeleton Lord stood watching, savoring the fear that the beasts so obviously showed. Then, with a swish of his elegant robe, he turned his attention to the opposite corner of the room.

The four stood, their hands gripping the bars, staring back at the Skeleton Lord. Even Anji dared to stare, unafraid, into the sardonic eyes.

"So, these are the new ones." The voice echoed silky and sibilant off the dungeon walls. "Including a Trans woman and a mere child." He turned to Leaal. "Why do you suppose they wandered about without permission in my desert? Just curious, or ulterior motives?"

"I'm not a child," Anji corrected. "I'm a young man." He glared at the Skeleton Lord.

"Ah, a spark of courage," the Skeleton Lord lisped. "I hate courage. He should be interesting when we break him."

"Leave the boy alone," Petia said hotly.

"Another ember there, my goodness. We do have a lively group here. Entertaining times are in store for us, Leaal."

Keja rattled the bars. "Just let us out of here, and we'll show you how entertaining."

The Skeleton Lord merely raised his thin, darkly arched eyebrows. He turned his attention to Giles. "And a quiet one. In my experience, I find the quiet ones . . . disquieting. He may be the most dangerous of all. We shall see. Enough,

Leaal. I must return to my work. I will question them later. Personally."

He turned, his robe swirling, and headed for the door. The hunchback pulled it open on squeaking hinges, bowing low to the Skeleton Lord. Leaal gave one last glance at the prisoners, whispered something to the gaoler, and followed his master out of the door.

A day passed before the Skeleton Lord's counselor arrived at the dungeon accompanied by six guards. He strode up and down the room, smiling as the beasts cowered in one corner of the cage. Leaal stood before the cage, enjoying the fear his mere presence had instilled in them. Finally he turned his attention to the humans.

Giles watched him suspiciously. The man had not come to the dungeon for petty maliciousness.

"Which of you is the leader?" Leaal asked.

"We have no leader," Keja said. "We consult the gods and let them choose our course."

Leaal's lip curled in disdain. "Do not try to tell such lies. It will do you no good. One of you is the leader. It is not the Trans bitch or the child. It must be one of you men. But which?"

"Go play with the hunchback," Giles said. He knew he risked much by angering Leaal, but he had to see how the man responded. Only by probing for weakness might they all escape.

A tremor ran through Leaal's body, and blood rushed to his face. "You are the leader."

He stepped back, gesturing to the gaoler to open the cage. The six guards stood with their spears ready. When the cage door swung open, Leaal pointed at Giles. "You, the old one, come out."

Giles had no choice but to obey. Petia reached up and touched his arm in reassurance. He ducked under the low door, and the skeleton men immediately surrounded him.

Leaal spun and marched out of the dungeon. One skeleton guard prodded Giles with a spear, and he followed, wondering if he would ever see his friends again.

Once out of the subterranean level, they entered wide, well-lighted hallways. The narrow stairways, however, gave no chance to escape. In a fight, Giles thought, only two guards would be able to control the stairwell. Giles smiled. That reduced the odds facing him, too.

The route twisted and turned. They climbed so many stairways that Giles soon lost track of how many levels they had climbed—seven?

At last, Leaal paused in front of a leather-covered door and then entered. Giles found himself in a large chamber. To his right was an archway and through it a smaller room. Glassware, candles, elaborate paraphernalia, bound books and loose parchments covered two large tables.

It was exactly as Giles had envisioned an alchemist's laboratory. What experiments did the Skeleton Lord do here? What did he search for? Some hidden knowledge that would add to his power? Wealth? Perhaps he, like other alchemists the world over, attempted to develop the elixir of flight.

Leaal stepped to the archway and bowed slightly. "Lord, the leader of the prisoners begs an audience."

The Skeleton Lord came through the archway, wiping bony fingers on a white linen cloth. When he had finished his minor ablutions, he flung the rag negligently back into the workroom. The rolled-up sleeves of his gown revealed blue stains on the underside of his arms.

Giles took the opportunity to study the desert lord more closely. When he had first heard of the Skeleton Lord, he had anticipated a skeletal being. The man was tall and slender almost to the point of emaciation, but the frame held firm human flesh and muscle. The face was wrinkled, the cheeks sunken. Thin wisps of white hair escaped from beneath the maroon robe's hood. Dark eyes stared out from sunken sockets with a bright madness in them.

The Skeleton Lord walked past Giles to take his seat on an elaborately carved wooden throne. He pointed to the floor in front of him, and Giles found himself thrust onto his knees before the ruler.

"Why are you here?" The Lord's thin voice grated on Giles' very soul.

"Because your men captured me and brought me here."

"Do not be clever, white-skinned one. My men will flay you alive if I so much as lift my finger. What were you and your party doing in my desert?"

Giles had had a day to think of the answer to this inevitable question. "In my land, we heard that immense riches could be gained from trading in the desert countries. We had thought to reopen the old caravan way, the Track of Fourteen, for trade between Kasha and Kuilla and the cities of the eastern coast, Hamri and Masser."

"Did no one tell you that this territory is forbidden? Did you not find dead caravaners along the way? I am the lord of all the desert between the coast and the caravan road, between Kasha and Kuilla. The old road will not be reopened. I do not wish it."

"But, of course, I am prepared to pay a tariff to the city of Shahal," Giles said. "It would be a pleasant place for the caravan to rest."

"I do not believe you. You have come to spy on me, to steal my secrets. I wield the power in this desert. My warriors obey me, and through them, the tribes of the desert. Why have you stirred up the beasts against me?"

"I met them in the desert. They told me that they could guide me to Shahal. I am unfamiliar with the desert, so I accepted their help."

The Skeleton Lord leaned forward. "They roam the desert because I will it. They did not deserve so fine a city; I banished them from it. They know better than to come back to Shahal."

"They did not tell me that." Giles tried to look confused and appalled at his breach of etiquette.

"Lies! You tell one lie on top of another. I will turn you and all your party into djinn and let you roam the desert with the beasts. But torture first. You must be punished so that you will not repeat the same stupid mistake—and to serve as an example to others of your ilk. When I am finished with you, you will know who is lord." The Skeleton Lord pointed his finger at Giles.

"But we have done nothing—"

"Silence! I have much work to do. I have gathered the power of the desert to me. But there are other cities that will come under my power. Eventually the entire continent. All Bandanarra will be mine. Nobody will interfere with my plan."

Giles glanced toward the archway into the smaller room. "You intend to use magic to do that?"

"Take a close look at my guards, foreign fool," the Skeleton Lord said. "Once they were men like you, but I have transformed them into invincible skeletons with my magic. They require no water or food, need no sleep and can fight harder than a dozen men! And my armies will grow!"

Giles watched as the madness surfaced in the Skeleton Lord. The pupils of his eyes grew larger and his hands shook as he gestured.

"Be careful, animal lover, or you will find yourself and your friends in my skeleton army. As a djinn you will be free—to roam the desert. Do not cooperate and you will become a part of my army, without eyes or flesh or emotions."

Giles bowed his head, placating the Lord with false obeisance. The time for open rebellion had not yet come.

"Take him away. I will deal with him later. Return him to the cells."

The cacophony of thoughts disturbed Petia. She used her empathic talent sparingly, projecting only when she needed to, and then at great mental and physical cost. Contacting Sleek had exhausted her; Giles' request to study Djinn had been virtually impossible except for the strongest of emotions.

But she knew now that it was the gaoler's mind that interfered with her thoughts. The poor old man had been in this dungeon over long and had not seen a woman in years. Even in his youth, his misshapen body had left him without voluntary female companionship. Now he lived in this dungeon, as much a prisoner as those he watched, merely a vassal of the Skeleton Lord. He found no joy in his work. He was hated by those he kept, abused by the guards he occasionally saw, despised by Leaal, ignored by the Skeleton Lord.

She read his emotions easily. The old man lusted to touch her. At first Petia was embarrassed, but she gradually realized there was nothing sexual in his thoughts about her. To him she was so beautiful that simply to touch her hand or face would be enough. While she felt sorry for him, Petia knew that she might be able to use the old man for their own purposes.

Carefully, slowly, so as not to disturb the old man, at great emotional cost to herself, Petia implanted simple thoughts into his mind, primitive emotions into his soul. The gaoler's befuddled mind followed her reasoning easily: These prisoners were not a danger and had not screamed filth at him.

Petia quaked and turned deathly pale as she erased fear from the man's brain and tried to keep her own desperation from intruding.

He had no reason to believe that they would do him harm if he let them out for just a little while, Petia instructed. He could easily put them back into their cage before the guards came to check the dungeon each morning and night. The Skeleton Lord will praise him for the good job he was doing.

Petia gently urged the gaoler over to the cage. Hesitantly, he approached and looked at the four prisoners. Petia smiled.

"There is so little room in this cage," she said. "It would feel so good to stretch."

"I . . . Teloq let you out for a short time," the gaoler said. "But you would have to go back in when I say. If the guards find you out, I will be whipped. You must promise Teloq."

"We wouldn't want you to get into trouble," Petia purred, her yellow catlike eyes gleaming with triumph. "You have been so kind to us. You are our friend. We promise you." She looked sternly at Giles and Keja, even as she supported herself against the bars.

"Friend," Teloq repeated. "I am your friend." He reached for the keys to the door of the cage. Before he got the key into the lock, the click of boots against stone echoed through the passageways. The gaoler jerked back, the tenuous spell Petia held over him broken.

The hunchback bowed low as Leaal strode into the dungeon and silently pointed at Keja. After Teloq opened the door, skeleton warriors pulled the small thief from the cell and jerked him around, easily holding him no matter how hard he struggled.

When Keja returned, his anger boiled over. "Giles, you bastard! You've deserted to the enemy!" He turned to Petia. "Don't believe a thing he says. I don't know what the Skeleton Lord has promised him but he sold us out."

"What are you talking about?" A dangerous softness edged in his voice.

"You said that you didn't trust us," Keja said. "We're the ones who shouldn't have trusted you. The Skeleton Lord bought you. At what price?"

Petia intervened. "What do you mean? What has Giles done? Quit talking in circles."

Keja seethed. "Giles promised to help him in his experiments. That's what the Skeleton Lord told me. He's searching for greater magicks. What did he offer you, Giles?"

"Don't be more of a fool than you have to be, Keja." Giles forced calmness upon himself. "It must be true," he finally said.

"What?" demanded Keja. "What's true?"

"That it's easy to dupe a thief. The Skeleton Lord sucked you in completely with his lies."

Petia stepped between the two men. "It's what the Skeleton Lord hoped, Keja. He told you lies, and sent you back here so enraged at Giles that you're ready to fight. It's the oldest ploy in the world." She took hold of Keja's wrists. "Sit down and be still. Then we'll listen to what the Skeleton Lord told you."

"What could he offer me, Keja? The key? We've traveled thousands of miles to find the next key. Do you think I told him about the Gate to Paradise? 'Just give me the key and I'll help you with your magicks'? Sometimes you don't think any better than he does." Giles jerked his head at the hunchback. "I told you last night what he said. All threats. He didn't even ask to bargain for our help. He promised torture, transformation into a djinn, and banishment into the desert. I don't know what he's trying to do to us, but Petia's right. It's a stratagem that's been used since the world began."

Keja said nothing, glaring at Giles.

"But this goes deeper than the Lord's lies. You *wanted* to believe him, Keja. Why? You've been sullen and withdrawn for some time. Since out in the desert."

For a long time Keja sat alone, stewing. "I resent your always telling us what to do," he said. "Even worse, you're usually right. No one's ever told me what to do in my life."

"Always the lone warrior," said Giles, sighing. "You'll either come to trust the rest of us or we're going to die. The only way we can escape is together. Individual effort won't do it for us."

"Petia's emotion-tapping—" Keja began. Petia slapped her hand across his mouth to keep the gaoler from over-hearing. Teloq shuffled around, glancing in occasionally, his attention mostly on Petia.

"It exhausted her," Giles said. "We would have to carry her from the cell if she succeeded. Forcing ideas into *that* head isn't easy for her." He sighed. "Forcing ideas into *your* head's no easier."

"The Lord made it sound so plausible," Keja said.

"He's a masterful liar," said Giles.

From across the corridor came Red Mane's mournful howling. "He speaks the truth, human. The Skeleton Lord talked us out of our home. Shahal is rightfully ours!"

The brief outburst brought the gaoler back. He prodded Red Mane until the beast subsided and huddled in the rear of his cell, whimpering.

"Try it again," Keja urged Petia. "Make him let us out."

Before Petia could answer, the sound of soldiers marching filled the dungeon. Leaal came in, a sneer on his face.

"The Lord has no more use for them. Take them all out—for the experiment!"

Skeletal hands grabbed Giles and the others and pulled them out of their cell. What little time they'd thought remained had evaporated.

Chapter Twelve

Giles Grimsmate would not go to his death at the hands of an alchemist and torturer this easily. He jerked free of the skeletal hands gripping his arm and struck out. Bones rattled and pulled back, but the powerful hold on his arm stayed.

"Fight, Keja!" he called. "You wanted to before. Do it now!" The memory of the Skeleton Lord's laboratory burned too brightly in Giles' brain for him to do anything else but struggle now. But the bony warriors proved their worth; they overwhelmed him.

As they began dragging him from the chamber, Leaal said in a choked voice, "Stop. I . . . I am wrong. The Lord doesn't want them. None of them."

Giles wrenched around and saw the expression on Leaal's face. Never had he seen a man more frightened. But of what? This time Giles did not protest as the skeleton warriors thrust him back into the cage. If anything, he felt as if he'd come home safely.

Keja hung on the bars, glaring. The troops marched smartly from the dungeon, Leaal following. Sweat beaded the counselor's forehead and his eyes darted wildly, seeking ghosts that never appeared to any save himself.

"I don't know what happened, but something changed his mind," said Giles. He heard a whimpering noise and turned to find Anji huddled beside Petia. The Trans boy shook Petia, who sat with unseeing eyes.

"Petia!" Giles cried.

"I'm all right, Giles. So weak. Head spins. Dark, too. But it worked! I convinced Leaal that taking us signed his death warrant, too."

Giles saw that her strength returned slowly after her ordeal. Somehow, using her emotion-tapping talents, she had ignited true fear in Leaal and frightened the man away. What awful terrors had she unleashed in that maggoty pit of his mind? Giles shuddered, not wanting to know.

"Then our reprieve is only temporary. When the Lord doesn't find us staked out for his experiment, he'll either send Leaal back—or Leaal's replacement."

"How are we to escape now? Can you persuade the gaoler?" asked Keja. He stared down with some concern at Petia.

"I . . . I don't think so. My head feels as if it explodes constantly. Just moving about makes me giddy. To touch Teloq so soon after Leaal? No." Petia turned even paler at the thought.

"There's a chance we can trick him without using Petia," Giles said. "If we get out, do we free the beasts, too?"

Keja looked across to where Red Mane and the others still cowered. "They are no help. How I wish we could just turn into puffs of mist like Djinn. We could slip through the bars and be off in a flash."

"By the way, where's Djinn? I haven't seen him since the troops marched on us along the valley rim." Giles jumped a foot when the voice came next to his ear.

"Right here." Gradually the djinn materialized. "I told you that you have to call for me, or I go back to my ethereal state. I've been here all along, listening to your discussion. Just being quiet and awaiting your call. This is a fine dilemma facing you, if I might say so."

"Is your material body as strong as it looks?" Petia asked, eyeing the bulging shoulders and biceps.

"I don't have anything to compare it to, and I haven't done any real work for untold years, not that I did much while in real human form. But the muscles seem to stay the same, whether I exercise or not."

"Can you do anything to help us out of here, Djinn?" Keja asked.

"I could put the old fellow in a trance. His mind's none too sharp, or so it seems from here."

Four voices raised in incredulous unison. "You could?"

"Easily. His mind is so simple. I couldn't with the Skeleton Lord, though. Nor the skeleton guards. They're mindless."

Giles rubbed his forehead. "If you could do that, why didn't you do it to us when we trapped you in the goatskin?"

"Djinn lose their power when entirely enclosed. Why? I can't really say because I have never considered the point overly important. Crawling into a bottle and pulling in the plug behind you isn't something you do every day by accident."

Giles said, "If we can reach the Skeleton Lord's chambers and destroy his grimoires, perhaps even his experiments, we might take away some of his magical powers. I think that's what we should attempt first."

"It's the key we're after," Keja said. "Let's just find it and get out."

"We ought to let the beasts out," Petia said. "We can't leave them caged up like that."

"Why not?" Giles scowled. "They haven't done a thing for us. All those promises out in the desert and their talk about wanting their city back. They've got part of it. We don't have time, and as poorly as they fight, it'd be dangerous for us."

"While you folks talk this out, do you want me to open the door?" Djinn asked. Giles made an impatient gesture. Djinn made an elegant wave of his hand. Across the room, Teloq put his head to the table and snored loudly. Djinn flowed through the bars, rematerialized and picked up the proper key. In the wink of an eye, he freed the four.

Suddenly the old man sat up on his bench, staring straight ahead of him. Djinn frowned and shrugged, saying, "Losing my touch. Been a long time since I had a mind to work with."

"We noticed," grumbled Keja. But the djinn put the gaoler back into the trance. Before Teloq's old head touched the table again, Giles had retrieved their weapons from the wall racks.

Armed again, they felt ready to face whatever they might find outside. Keja pulled the door leading up and out of the dungeon. In spite of his care, it creaked and groaned. Keja grimaced, but Giles laid a hand on his arm in reassurance.

"Wait," came Red Mane's plaintive cry. "You can't leave us!"

"We're going scouting," Keja said. "You'll be safe here."

"But . . ."

Giles and Keja didn't look back at the beasts, and Petia only glanced at Red Mane. Keja was right in thinking the beasts were less likely to have danger befall them here than if they plundered about.

Steps led upward directly from the dungeon. The companions paused at the bottom, listening intently. Giles tried desperately to remember what the hallway above looked like, but nothing came. He and Keja started up the stairs, but Keja signed for Giles to wait. He closed the dungeon door and locked it behind him.

They advanced to the first turn and paused. Nothing appeared ahead of them. They moved to the top of the stairs. Giles cautioned them with his hand signal, then peered around the corner and down the hallway. Guards stood motionless at each end.

"Can we get around the corner into the next stairway?" Petia whispered from behind.

"No, the stairs don't go up from here," Giles answered. "It's a ways down the hall. Djinn, can't you put them in a trance?" Giles whispered.

"No, they are already locked in one more powerful than I can cast. When they were transformed, they lost the power of thinking for themselves. They respond automatically to signals known only to the Lord. I can't put them to sleep."

"Then we'll have to fight our way through?"

"Yes. Be on the watch for other beings that the Lord has. There are ghouls, seirim and dakari. Ghouls you must run from. The seirim are big, hairy creatures, but they are slow of foot and hand. Cut them in the legs, and be wary of their blood—it burns human flesh. The dakari are hideous females who roam the city at night, crying for their infants who the Lord killed."

"Thanks for the warning," Giles said. With such a panoply arrayed against them, simply getting out of Shahal presented insurmountable problems. How were they to find the key they so avidly desired? "Ready?"

Taking a breath, they stepped in unison into the hall and walked quietly, hoping to cover some ground between the two guards and themselves before discovery.

They nearly made it. Giles was only ten feet away when the first guard turned. In complete and eerie silence, the guard raised his spear. Giles covered the ten feet separating them in two strides, thumbing his sword. The blade took the guard in the spinal column before the spear leveled. Keja bowled the second guard over with his shoulder, then ran his blade through him. The guard paused, as if unsure of what happened, then continued his attack. Keja had to cut the legs from under the skeleton warrior, then sever head from torso before it stopped fighting.

Giles gave Keja no time to catch his breath. Giles gestured Petia and Anji up the stairwell. Petia stooped and picked up a short, curved sword. It felt heavier than her own sword, and she let it fall. Pulling Anji's arm, she scurried up the stairwell. Giles and Keja closed behind them. The guards from the far end of the hall were coming to investigate. By the time they reached the two dead skeleton men, the humans had reached the next floor.

They paused briefly to see where the guards were stationed, then dashed around the corner and up another flight. It seemed wiser to elude the guards than to fight from floor to floor. Sooner or later the guards would catch up with them.

The third level was empty. "Where are the guards?" Petia whispered. They saw none in front of them or at the far end of the corridor.

Giles stepped gingerly into the hallway. He cupped his ear and listened intently. Quiet. He was turning to motion to the others when he heard a clicking sound on the floor behind him. He spun around with an oath and brought his sword up.

Keja stepped up the last stair and into the hall, ready to face the implacable skeleton guards coming from their right. He blanched.

"What did we do to deserve this?" he gasped.

A mass of scorpions scuttled down the short corridor toward them. Their bodies stood two feet tall, and tails curling wickedly above their backs added another foot. The carapaces of their segmented bodies gleamed like lacquered boxes and were spotted with glistening fluid that sizzled and popped—poison dripping from the tail barb. And those tails! Taut, they weaved from side to side, ready to strike.

Petia came up into the hall and gasped. She pushed Anji to one side and took a position on Giles' left, her shorter sword ready.

The eerie clicking sound made it hard to estimate how many of the arachnids were approaching. The tight mass of deadly creatures flowed like a living carpet, but Giles counted at least ten deadly, waving tails.

"Remember," he yelled. "It's their tails. Slice them off. By all the gods, don't let them get you with that stinger."

"Stay behind me, Anji," Petia called over her shoulder.

"Give me your short sword, Mistress."

"No, stay back."

Then the scorpions erupted over them. Giles thrust at the beady black eye of the center one, and it backed away. Petia swung her sword in an arc, cutting through the tail of one scorpion and followed down to slice through the carapace. The scorpion was driven to the floor and lay dying, feebly waving its front legs. Petia had to fight to pry free her blade from the carcass.

Keja stamped on the floor, momentarily startling the arachnids, then leaped forward, extending one leg and his sword arm. The sword tip slid between the eye and the center of the scorpion's head. He pulled it out with a vicious twisting motion as he leaped back. He did not have time to watch the ichorous matter oozing from its head, nor to see it drop, twitching to the floor. Already another attacked and demanded his full attention.

"Do these things ever die?" Petia cried. Her blade glanced off armored carapace as she spoke. Giles grasped his sword in both hands, feeling the energy emanating from it. He leaped forward, swinging it like a broadsword. The sword lopped a scorpion's tail cleanly. It fell with a rattle against the wall, saving Petia a nasty wound.

"That's three," he murmured grimly.

Petia started to thank him, then heard Anji cry. While she had been busy with one arachnid, another had scuttled past her. It headed for Anji, who backed away. Petia spun and leaped after it. With a surge of frenzied energy, she swung the sword in two connected arcs, the first severing the tail, the second decapitating the creature. Without looking, she swung around again to face another scurrying toward her.

Gingerly, Anji picked up the severed tail. It dripped with the venom that had been intended for him. A grim, small smile crossed his lips. If Petia would not give him a sword, he'd use the severed tail and join the battle.

He ran forward, focusing clearly on one scorpion sidling toward Giles. With an audible cry, he plunged the stinger into the unsuspecting scorpion's eye. It turned quickly, tail wavering, and collapsed at Anji's feet.

"Anji," Petia cried. "Get back. That's an order."

Five scorpions remained to menace the humans. The ugly creatures scurried from side to side, looking for a chance to strike. Giles drew back, taking the opportunity to catch his breath. The danger would not be over until the scorpions retreated or were killed.

And even then . . .

For a moment, the scorpions seemed to hesitate, then rose on short back legs, front feet wavering. They acted as if they awaited instructions.

Keja yelled, "Now!" He rushed forward, sword aimed low. He thrust upward into the brittle underbelly, pulling his sword upward as he withdrew it. Giles and Petia took his meaning instantly and followed. Petia pulled her sword from a scorpion, already thinking of her next move. Without stopping, she slashed to her left and then back to the right. The scorpion backed away, but it was too late. The tip of the sword swept across its eyes. It scuttled blindly into the wall, then turned sightlessly. Keja neatly severed its tail, recovered and sliced it in two.

Keja feinted at the single remaining scorpion, got its attention with a second feint, and withdrew. As the arachnid followed, Giles neatly sliced its head off from the side.

"That's all?" Giles asked, still stunned by their arachnid attackers. He thumbed the inscription and relaxed as the energy drained from his sword. They leaned on their weapons, breathing deeply and examining the carnage in front of them. Two of the scorpions still twitched feebly. Petia made a gagging sound and leaned against the wall.

Looking down the empty hall, Giles decided they had time to rest. He put his arm on Petia's shoulder. "She'll be all right in a moment," he said to Anji. He looked around to congratulate Keja.

Keja had vanished.

Petia ran her hand through her tangled, filthy hair, pushing it out of her eyes. She wiped the perspiration from her forehead. "That was horrible," she said. "But we did it. Can we get out of here? The sight of those awful creatures makes me sick."

Nodding curtly, Giles motioned for her to stay a pace back while he scouted the stairs. They were a half flight up when Petia stumbled and fell.

"Giles, it's Keja. I heard him."

"I heard nothing," Giles said, thinking she had lost her mind. If anything, the terrible silence gnawed at his courage.

"I heard Keja with my mind. He let out an emotional cry for help. He's frightened. Scared out of his mind. I *feel* it!"

"Keja in trouble is nothing new," said Giles. "He knew better than to run off by himself."

"He's found a treasure room, but he's trapped by a giant snake. Hurry. The images are clouded by his fear." She turned paler by the instant.

"The fool. Why couldn't he stay with us?" Giles scowled. He turned the corner of the half landing and halted, stumbling back into Petia and Anji. Two guards, spears ready, came down the steps. Giles thumbed the sword. "If we're to reach Keja, we fight," he said.

Petia took her stance besides him, sword at the ready.

Again, Keja's mental shout came. She trembled visibly. She thrust it away to concentrate on the enemy ahead of her. Keja would have to act on his own. But he intruded so in her mind!

The skeleton men advanced with measured steps. When their spears were just beyond the humans, Petia swept her sword to the left, engaging the shaft of one spear and driving it aside. On her return she slashed the guard's legs. His legs buckled, and Giles stepped up to drive his sword through the man. This only slowed the skeleton warrior; Giles recovered and decapitated the guard.

The second guard had time to sweep down at Giles with his spear. Petia stepped inside the blow and deflected it,

giving Giles the opportunity to cleave head from torso
—the only sure way of stopping the skeleton warriors.

The skeleton dropped the spear and put his hands to his
neck, then seemed to decide the fight had ended for him.
The skeleton twisted around and crashed noisily to the
floor.

Keja's cries were audible to Giles when they reached the
top of the stairs. Petia pointed down the corridor. A
doorway halfway down the long hall stood open.

A seething mass of adders filled the doorway. Petia
glanced beyond and saw Keja standing atop a mound of
treasure. A huge viper slid toward him.

Giles skidded to a stop beside her. The adders were
between them and the interior of the room. They unwound
themselves and quickly formed ranks, threatening to encir-
cle them.

"Get me out of here!" screamed Keja. "I *hate* snakes!"
His sword thrusts were erratic and driven by fear, not skill.
Giles saw Keja would soon perish unless they could rescue
him.

But how? Killing all the snakes looked like an impossible
task. For every one that vanished behind a gaudy trinket,
two more appeared from chests or from small holes in the
walls.

The tip of Giles' sword wavered. "First scorpions and
now adders. The Skeleton Lord has more in his arsenal than
just skeleton men, doesn't he?"

Giles gathered his wits and courage, ready to make the
run through the snakes. If he joined Keja, together they
might fight their way free.

Maybe. Giles doubted it. There were too many adders.

But he had to try. He let out a loud cry and rushed
forward, sword swinging this way and that, slashing through
yielding snake parts.

Chapter Thirteen

*T*he first adder struck and missed. Giles jumped, bumping Petia. "Sorry," he said. "We've got to work together and forge a trail. You and Anji go right, I'll take the left. Go!"

His sword swept back and forth, inches above the floor, dealing death at every swing. He severed heads, cut bodies in half until the floor was littered with writhing segments of adder. The reptiles didn't realize that they were dead, and continued to slither.

Giles forged forward powerfully—and the living snakes began retreating. Of the dead—those that would finally die at midnight—Giles watched even more carefully. He yelled in triumph, "Keja! Hurry! We've made a path for you!"

Slipping and sliding atop the mound of jewels, Keja faced a viper so large it paralyzed the thief with fear. The enormous snake measured fully a sword's width across the mouth, and its fangs rivaled Keja's sword for length and sharpness. As the man backed off, the reptile wove its way ponderously among the treasures. Keja had no way to escape. Inexorably, the snake forced him to the wall.

He took a step backward, slipped on a cuirass. The armor tipped and Keja sat down in the midst of a king's ransom.

The snake reared, preparing for the death stroke. Keja's eyes widened, and fear locked any but the smallest of cries deep in his throat. But when death came, it was to the snake and not the man.

Giles' glowing sword met one fang and chipped it off. A second powerful swing engaged the second snake fang. By the time the ponderous reptile swung to see who dared attack it, Giles had found the spot—he thrust true. The giant viper jerked about the sword spitting it, its huge length smashing priceless artwork to dust.

By the time Giles pulled his sword, Keja had recovered.

141

Ashen-faced, he simply stared at the carcass.

"Come on!" cried Petia. "Guards!" She paused at the door of the room. Mounds of treasure winked out at her. Jewels sparkled, reflecting the dim light from the corridor. Goblets of gold, ropes of chalcedony and pearl, pendants of sapphire and emerald tempted her. But Petia let the treasure remain. Too much weight to carry.

Anji seconded her warning: "Guards, they're coming down the hall."

Petia sprang to the boy's side. She saw skeleton warriors advancing on them and, for a moment, she felt relieved. These were known dangers, not immense snakes or hideous scorpions. Anji clutched a ceremonial short sword he had recovered from the treasure trove.

The guards walked stiffly down the hall, automatons obeying an unheard order. Petia held her sword and another, shorter one she'd picked up. "Anji, you stay out of this."

"No, Mistress."

"And I freed you. Don't call me 'Mistress.' "

He did not move from her side. Four skeleton men advanced. Behind them, four more stood ready.

Giles sprang to the door and thrust Anji back. "Where's Djinn?" he muttered to himself.

"Here, Giles," Djinn responded. "What a noble battle. Reminds me of my own days when I sported a body. What great fun then, yes, great fun."

Giles kept his eyes on the skeleton men, but out of the side of his mouth he said, "Where have you been?"

"I've been here. You've got to remember to call me. I vanish, otherwise. It's the way of djinn."

"We've got to find some place to hide, somewhere to rest. Find it, then report back."

Djinn bowed. "I hear and obey, O master."

He disappeared, and Giles yelled, "Keja, where are you? We've got eight guards out here."

"I lost my sword and am looking for it," came the answer.

"Hurry up!" Giles sprang at the skeleton man nearest Petia, giving her precious seconds to ready herself. Petia parried a spear thrust, letting it slide by her. She swung her sword hard and low. Her blade caught the warrior just below the knee. He stumbled and fell, blood oozing feebly from the desiccated leg bone. She forgot about him and went on to the next skeleton man.

Giles slashed at the first one and was surprised when the guard dodged to avoid the blade. Never before had he seen one retreat, so little did their ersatz lives mean to them —and so strong was the Skeleton Lord's spell.

Feeling someone approaching from the rear, Giles spun to meet the aggressor. Keja, still pale from his ordeal, staggered away from the doorway. He carried a gaudy jewel-encrusted sword, but it looked sturdy enough for a fight. "The small snakes have returned to the treasure room," he said.

Then he screamed and leaped between Petia and Giles, smashing his sword against a spear. Before the skeleton man could recover, Keja lifted his sword above his head and sliced down on the exposed head. The sword rebounded from hard bone. The guard brought his spear back and thrust at Keja. He spun to the right and the spear grazed the side of his body.

"That does it," Keja muttered.

He waded in, slicing right and left, making contact with every swing. He didn't care what he hit. Arms, legs, rib cages felt the force of his blow. The dull sword broke bones. Keja paid no attention and hacked away like a demon.

Giles and Petia ducked away from Keja's maddened, wild swings, taking care not to be caught by an errant blow. They found themselves behind the second rank of guards. Petia raised her sword with both hands and angled it down against a neck. The guard dropped, his spear clattering against the wall. Giles thrust through a spine, feeling the hum of his sword destroy the skeletal being.

When they looked up, no guards were left to fight. Keja leaned on his sword, puffing and blowing. The anger slowly left his face to be replaced by a childlike smile. "Bring on some more," he said.

"No," Giles said. "We need to rest. Djinn, where are you?"

Halfway down the hall, Djinn materialized, beckoning to them. Petia pushed Anji ahead of her down the corridor. Giles gripped Keja's shoulder. "Come on," he said.

Keja sucked in a deep breath. "Got to get my own sword. You sure that snake is dead?" He peered cautiously into the room. The viper's tail still writhed feebly. He edged past it and, ignoring the smaller snakes, quickly retrieved his weapon. Then he fled after his companions.

"There are nooks and crannies all over this place," Djinn said. "What a delightful place to play at scavenger hunt. Guards come by occasionally. They'll be poking their noses everywhere soon, but I found a room that looks like it hasn't been used for a long time."

He rounded a corner, took a few steps and opened a door. It groaned but opened wide enough for them to enter. Giles leaned his weight against it and closed it.

Light filtered into the room from an embrasure far above. Giles narrowed his eyes to examine the interior. Some sacking lay against one wall, but otherwise the room appeared empty.

"I wish we had a candle," Petia whispered in the half light. "I've had enough snakes for one day."

Giles held his sword ready, made a tour around the room and found nothing. He congratulated Djinn on his fine work.

"I guess we can relax," said Keja. He lowered himself onto the sacking and rested his head against the wall. He closed his eyes and murmured, "I didn't realize how tired I was."

"That's from going berserk," Giles said. He had never seen Keja in such a rage before. He wondered what really powered the sudden fury.

"Djinn?"

The djinn materialized with a loud *pop!* behind Giles.

"I wish you'd quit doing that. You give me the shivers. I want you to go to the dungeon and release the beasts. Send them back into the desert. They aren't going to be of any help to us, but there's no sense in them rotting away down there. Then come back here. If you ever hope to be changed back into a human, you've got to help us."

"Ah," he said knowingly, "the key, is it? But I will do anything to regain my human body." The djinn disappeared instantly.

Petia slumped to the floor, gesturing to Anji to sit beside her. She was worried. She had expected skeleton men but not the slithering and chittering creatures that the Skeleton Lord flung against them. She hadn't worried about Anji during their trip through the desert; that had been his home as a slave. But she had not counted on the dangers confronting them now. She liked the boy, and the awesome responsibility for him had finally hit her. He wasn't her own son—but he could have been. Petia couldn't bear to see Anji hurt, much less killed.

Thinking, Giles paced the room for a time. He glanced at Keja: fast asleep. Petia and Anji talked quietly but with great emotion. The responsibility of command fell heavily on Giles. It was hard enough with two thieves like Petia and Keja—they didn't need an eleven-year-old to watch. But where lay the answer? He settled down across from Keja and stretched out. Gradually his heart slowed. The images of scorpions and snakes dimmed. He and the others would stay hidden here, getting needed sleep and regaining their strength. Then . . .

Giles slept.

Djinn made his way down to the dungeon, glancing down the hallway of each floor. Already the bodies of skeleton men, snakes and scorpions had been removed.

When he reached the large iron door, he became a mere wisp and drifted through the spy hole. Teloq sat in a stupor behind his table.

Djinn glanced across the room. The beasts were still in their cage in one corner. They looked despondent, as if even hope had fled.

The old gaoler reached to a corner of the table and picked up a bottle; unsteadily he poured it into a battered cup. Djinn felt sorry for him. Teloq didn't have much of a life, even less now that he had let prisoners escape. Solace from a bottle. Djinn understood.

Drifting over, Djinn saw that the old man had drunk himself into a stupor. In his condition the gaoler posed no threat.

Floating to the beast's cage, Djinn materialized. "Red Mane," he whispered.

"Who's there?" The tawny beast came to the front of the cage.

"I've come to free you. Giles says I'm to get you out of Shahal and into the desert. Then you're on your own."

Red Mane growled. "What do you mean, 'out into the desert'?" The other beasts crowded around him. He rubbed his hindquarters until they quieted.

"Giles says you're better off there than in a cage. He doesn't think you'll help. At first he was angry, but he decided not to let you languish down here. He told me to set you free."

"Why does he think we can't help?"

Djinn considered for a moment, then blurted, "The word he used was 'cowardice.'"

"What!" bellowed Red Mane. He spun and exposed his rump to Djinn in his anger. "We want our city back, and we will fight! We aren't going back to the desert. We'd rather die first. We swore an oath on it. Let us out of here and take us to Giles."

Djinn considered for a moment. "He didn't say anything about that."

"Never mind," Red Mane growled. "Just release us."

"You're going to need weapons," Djinn said. "I'll unlock the cage, but stay in it until I return. I'm going to check a treasure room and see if I can find any decent weapons there."

Red Mane waited impatiently. He turned to the other beasts. "Just remember what you promised. 'Cowards' he called us. If we want this city back, we've got to fight. Do you understand?"

All the beasts nodded.

Djinn returned and checked on poor old Teloq. He snored peacefully, head on the table.

As he opened the heavy iron door, Djinn beckoned the beasts. He whispered in Red Mane's ear, "The halls are empty, but I don't know how long they'll stay that way. There are weapons, not the best, but serviceable. Quickly now, follow me."

Within minutes they gained the stairs and slipped into the room Djinn had found for a hiding place.

Giles looked up, surprised at the number of beings

entering the room. "I told you to turn them loose in the desert."

Djinn, halfway changed to a vaporous wisp, lifted nearly immaterial hands in a gesture of futility.

Giles stared hard at Red Mane. "By the gods, you'd better fight this time. No more cowering in corners. It's side by side with us, or we'll turn on you ourselves."

Red Mane glared back. "Don't believe you have all the courage, human. We're determined. We want Shahal back and we mean to have it."

Petia held up her hand. "Shh. Someone's outside," she whispered.

Maniacal shouting carried down the corridor. "Find them, you scum. You've got to find them. Don't let them get away. Kill every last one of them."

"It's the Skeleton Lord's advisor," Anji whispered.

They heard the slow tread of the skeleton warriors marching past and Leaal's voice hounding them mercilessly. "Onward, you dolts. Find them and bring me their still beating hearts!" The voice faded down the corridor.

Then the storeroom door burst inward. They were discovered!

Chapter Fourteen

Giles blasted to his feet, sword ready. The beasts cowered, but Red Mane pressed close to Giles to lend aid against the intruder.

"The door," Petia started. Her voice died down.

Giles turned red with rage when he saw Djinn pushing against the door. The spirit creature laughed, trying to hide the sound behind a vaporous hand. "Oh, this was a good prank, so good!" he chortled. "The other djinn would approve. You were scared, weren't you?"

"Did any of the guards see you?" demanded Giles, his anger still not fully under control. He forced calmness on himself, but Djinn made it almost impossible.

"You worry over much," Djinn said. "They headed down the corridor, to search the far parts of Shahal." Djinn floated in front of Giles. "You are mad," he said, as if he'd never considered this possibility.

"For someone who depends on our aid, you tread dangerous ground," Giles said between clenched teeth.

Djinn looked confused and drifted to the side of the storeroom, then slowly faded to nothingness. Giles indicated the others should rest. He settled down, arms crossed. Soon the tension fled his body and he, too, slept.

Petia awoke to sunlight warming her face. She rolled over sleepily, then came fully alert when she couldn't find Anji. Petia's quick eyes took a poll of human and beast—Anji and Sleek were both missing.

She jerked to her feet and went to the door, peering out. Where had the boy gone? Giles would be furious at him for wandering off. *She* was mad at him, too!

Petia slipped into the corridor to find the youth. He couldn't have gone far.

* * *

Giles awoke to murmurs of concern from the beasts. He sat up, rubbing his eyes and pulling the tangles from his graying hair, wondering what caused the stir among them. It took him only seconds to discover three missing from the rank.

"When did they go?" Giles demanded, reaching for his sword.

"I don't know," Red Mane said. "They were gone when we awoke."

"Sometime during the night, probably," he mused. "Who had the idea first, I wonder?" He pulled himself to his feet and faced the beasts. "I'm going looking for them. I want you all to stay here. We don't have any chance if we keep splitting up and going off by ourselves."

He checked the hallway and slipped out. At the end of the corridor another hall crossed at right angles. He looked carefully around the corner—empty, stairways on either end.

He took them two at a time, stopping to check the next level. The passageway was empty. Giles turned the corner and hurried up another flight and into the arms of four skeleton men. He reached for his sword—too late. One guard gripped his forearm. The bony body had enormous strength in its arms and hands. Giles struggled, but the grip grew tighter.

In eerie silence, they carried him roughly up a flight of stairs to the Skeleton Lord's chamber. As they entered, the Skeleton Lord looked up, unsurprised, from his reeking flasks.

"Over there." He pointed to the corner. "Hold him firmly."

Burners and candles stood beneath some of the flasks. Liquids of various colors bubbled or simmered, but many of them were shades of red. Insidious odors permeated the room and tormented his nose. Wisps of vapor rose toward the discolored ceiling. Gases had condensed to liquid and streaked the wall with ugly blotches.

But the Skeleton Lord's attitude startled him. The Lord took scarce note of his presence, as if he were little more than a bug that had crawled into the laboratory. Giles watched the Skeleton Lord bend over a table to look at the contents of a beaker. It bubbled merrily, flinging an occasional droplet into the air. When they hit the table, they sizzled as if hitting a hot pan and vanished into a wisp of acrid smoke. Giles hoped that one would hit the man in the eye.

The Skeleton Lord continued down the table, examining the contents of his glassware. Occasionally he picked up a glass, peering at its bubbling contents. Others he sniffed, and once he dipped an elongated forefinger into the beaker, then tasted the liquid.

When he finished, he looked at Giles, as if wondering why the man stood there. Finally his eyes cleared and he said, "Guards. Stand to one side but be ready. If he attacks, kill him."

One gestured to another. The skeleton man shuffled forward, pulled a knife from his belt, and waited, ready.

The Skeleton Lord rounded the table, pulling a stool with him. He perched upon it to confront Giles.

He's nearly as thin as the men he has created, Giles thought. His eyes were sunken, the skin on his face unnaturally pale. It pulled over the cheekbones like a thin layer of parchment.

His robes hung loose, and Giles saw a scrawny portion of one leg showing. For all his power and abilities, the man wasted away to nothing. A good desert wind would pick him up and bury him in the Calabrashio Seas.

"Well." The thin reedy voice puzzled Giles. When he was questioned only a few days before, the voice had been strong and unwavering. What it might mean, Giles feared he would find out all too soon.

"Escaped from my cells, did you? And where are the rest of them? Even the beasts are gone, poor dumb things."

"You are the leader, even though you deny it," the Lord continued, his voice still weak. "The rest of them have no chance without you." Giles remained quiet, waiting for some clue to the Skeleton Lord's plan.

The Lord leaned forward, rheumy eyes studying Giles. "A military man, aren't you? It shows in your bearing. And a leader, too. I could use you."

Giles remained silent.

"Yes, I have need of a man like you," he mused. "My skeleton men need leadership. The Harifim are mine. But there is word of a black-robed stranger gathering men from the other tribes. I don't know what his intentions are, but I would rather be prepared."

Giles waited for his chance. It had to come. It had to.

"Those companions of yours," the Lord continued. "An unusual lot; unworthy of you. How did you come to throw in with them? Not the key, certainly." He looked slyly at Giles.

Giles blinked, his first defeat. How did the Lord know they sought the key to the Gate of Paradise?

"I know," he said confidently. "And I'll find your companions before long and kill them. But you can be useful to me. You could share power—a great deal of power—with me. With your military experience, I can take over the entire continent more quickly. You will lead the Harifim, be the tactician. They fight well but are undisciplined children. With me to lay out plans and you to lead them, we will sweep the desert! Then the towns. The continent will be ours!"

"I don't abandon my companions as easily as you think," Giles muttered. "And you'll never conquer the continent."

"You may not like it much," the reedy voice said. "But if you care so much for your friends, you may wish to save their skins." His eyes cleared for a moment, and Giles was surprised at the intensity shining forth. "For I will have your help, whether you want to or not.

"As for the key, it is useless without the others. Ah, you look surprised. Yes, there are others. The Gate of Paradise cannot be opened without them all."

Giles thought he hid his surprise well—and that he kept the Lord from guessing that the companions already had three keys in safekeeping.

"The Gate of Paradise," the Lord continued. "A tale, an old legend. There is no wealth or power there. I will have both here on Bandanarra. Do you not wish to share it with me?"

"Not especially," Giles answered. "I've had enough of war. I've killed enough people. I don't wish to kill any more." The skeleton men moved forward with their spears, pricking Giles in the chest.

"Sick of killing?" The Skeleton Lord looked surprised. "Why is that? Do you think that there is worth in a human? There is, as a matter of fact." He pointed at the beakers on the table. "Blood. Blood for my experiments. Human blood and animal blood. I have worked long to find its essence.

"When I succeed, I will be able to make my skeleton men live forever. I will make them more than the shambling beings they have become. They will be the scourge of the desert, the elite troops, leaders of the desert tribes. But I need more blood for my experiments. Even yours, if you don't cooperate."

"How long have you been holed up in this city of rock, working on your insane schemes, changing tribesmen into walking skeletons, seeking to find the power to rule the entire continent?" Giles hadn't meant to speak; the words leaped out before he could stop them.

The Skeleton Lord held up a beaker containing a viscous red substance. He dipped his finger into it, then licked it with his tongue. Disgusted, Giles averted his eyes.

"This is the essence of life," the Lord continued, as if he hadn't heard. "This is what will give me great power."

Giles stirred. "It doesn't give power when it drains away from men's bodies. I've watched it too many times. The slice of a sword and a man in great pain, watching himself die by inches. It's the same with your soldiers as it has been with soldiers all over the world."

"The blood of my men will be different!" the Skeleton Lord raged. "It will not seep away. It will stay within them, rebuilding the tissues, closing the wound."

"Your men will die exactly like other men. Your wonderful blood will not prevent that."

"No," the Lord screamed. "Not so. This blood is different." He dipped his hand into the beaker again. It came out red and dripping. "This is a fluid that will make men immortal. They will never die. You are wrong!"

Giles leaned back against the wall and watched the Skeleton Lord pace back and forth, mouthing his beliefs in his experiments. Giles wondered if there were any way to calm the man—or if he even wanted to try.

* * *

Keja waited anxiously. He wished he had some way of knowing how long Giles had been gone. The shaft of light from the high window had moved off the floor and several feet up the wall. Keja beat his fist against the wall.

"Pacing won't bring them back any sooner," said Red Mane. He patted the floor beside him.

Keja slumped to the floor with a sigh. "I know. But night is coming, and Giles has been gone all day. If he's not back by dark, I'm going looking for him."

"Would that be wise?" Red Mane asked. "He told us to stay here until he came back."

"We can't stay here until we're skeletons ourselves," Keja said. "Are you afraid? With you or without you, I'm leaving when it's dark."

"We're not afraid," Red Mane said, scowling. "We'll go with you and fight, whether it's wise or not. We know the city and you don't."

Keja sat in silence a while longer, then called, "Djinn." Once again Keja was disconcerted by the gradual materialization from spirit to flesh. "I'll never get used to that," he said again.

"How do you think I've felt all these years?" Djinn replied. "What can I do for you?" Settling on the floor, he sat cross-legged facing Keja and Red Mane.

"We need a scout," Keja said. "I should have thought of it sooner. If you'd stick around so we could see you we wouldn't forget that you're here."

"Sorry, it can't be helped," Djinn said. "It's the way djinn are. We have to be called."

"I want you to find Giles. Or any of the others. Petia, Anji and Sleek are out there, too. I want you to go to the Skeleton Lord's chambers and find out what he's doing."

"You're taking your life in your hands, Keja. At night the *pazuzi*, the wind demons, come out of the cliffs along the edge of the plain. They roam the halls and corridors. It's a game to them, but they are dangerous."

"We have to chance it," Keja said. "We can't sit here forever. If the others are alive, they need our help. If they're dead, we need to get out of Shahal. It's that simple."

Djinn faded and the wisp disappeared beneath the door.

"I hope we can change him back into a human," Keja said. "I can't take much more of that."

After an hour Djinn returned and did not bring good news. "I found no trace of Petia, Anji or Sleek. Giles is a captive in the Skeleton Lord's chambers. I tried to speak with him, but the Lord was raving. I had no opportunity to free Giles. He's unbound, but his sword is gone."

"We've got to attempt a rescue," Keja said. "What about the hallways?"

"Empty," Djinn replied. "The skeleton men leave the halls before the wind demons come, otherwise they'd be swept down the halls and right over the edge of Shahal's balconies."

"Then, now is the time to move," Keja said decisively. "Everybody, we're going to attack the Skeleton Lord's chamber and try to free Giles. Capture the Skeleton Lord, too, if we can."

Keja and the beasts moved quickly into the corridor. Keja gestured for Red Mane to take the lead. "You know the way," he whispered.

Red Mane led the way up the stairs, and they gained another floor without incident. He hesitated, checked the corridor and whispered to Keja, "Nothing in this hallway. Shall we go up? Two more floors to the Lord's chambers."

"Pause when you get to that floor. We'll take a moment to ready ourselves." Keja rubbed his hand nervously over his sword hilt. He felt as if he were stalking his first victim. He forced himself to be calm by thinking about what Giles might do in this situation—and it bothered him that Giles probably wouldn't be in it at all.

Rapidly they ascended the stairway. Keja stopped at the top. "This is the floor. We're attacking the Skeleton Lord's chamber. Djinn?"

"Here."

"Check for us. How many guards in the chamber, and how are they armed? I'm going to mutter your name until you get back so I can see you."

Djinn disappeared before Keja could even begin to utter his name. The spirit returned in a short time, appearing as he came within the sound of Keja's voice.

. "Four guards armed with spears," he reported. "One

commanding; he has a short sword."

Keja turned to the beasts. "We outnumber them. I'll take care of Giles. You attack the guards, but be careful of the Lord. There's no way to know if he can use his magicks against us quickly enough to matter."

He and the others started down the corridor at a trot. Suddenly, Red Mane put out his hand and stopped. Keja halted beside him.

"What is it?" he asked.

Then he heard the whisper of wind. It began softly, like someone blowing across the mouth of a jug. The tone sharpened. At the far end of the hall tapestries curled slightly at the edges, the fringe ruffling. The wind grew and the tapestries billowed out. The sound increased, and the wall hangings whipped about violently.

Behind him Keja heard a beast gasp, *"Pazuzi!"*

Chapter Fifteen

The wind demons roared down the corridor toward Keja. Air compressed ahead of the *pazuzi* and pushed powerfully at him. His eardrums almost exploded and his eyes watered.

"Where are they?" he yelled at Red Mane over the deafening rush.

"You cannot see them," Red Mane answered. "They are only wind. You see their effect, not their bodies."

"How do we fight them? How do we defend ourselves?" Keja shouted.

"You can't." Red Mane gestured to the other beasts. "We will protect you."

The force of a *pazuzi* staggered Keja. Recovering, he leaned into the gale, covering his eyes with his forearm. He yelled at Red Mane, but the wind ripped the words from his mouth. He could hear only a hurricane's roar. Red Mane put a finger to his ear and shook his head, but Keja could not see; his eyes poured tears.

A second wind demon hit Keja and whirled him in a circle. He spun like a child's top, crashing into a wall and spinning along it down the corridor. Keja screamed when he saw that only a low balustrade at the end of the hall protected him from falling five stories to the desert floor.

Red Mane made a circling gesture, and one shaggy long-limbed beast dropped to his hands and knees along the wall, directly in Keja's path. When Keja came within reach, the beast clasped the human around the waist. Two others grabbed the small thief's arms and pulled him to the center of the hall. Red Mane loomed over him to protect him from the wind demons' depredations.

The *pazuzi* screeched angrily, thwarted of their prey. Dozens of them roared down the hall, buffeting the circle of beasts, who calmly turned their backs to the fierce winds. The force and the chill of the *pazuzi* did not approach that of the desert. The beasts even welcomed it.

"Feel that?" Red Mane roared. "Is this our city? Do you remember?" He faced the *pazuzi*, raising his hands in a gesture both welcoming and challenging of the battle. A howl of acceptance came from the demons. They remembered the beasts. Gale forces whipped down the hall, creating turbulences deadly to creatures less powerful than the beasts. Had Keja's eyes been open he would have been dumbfounded at the grins that creased the mouths of the beasts. They enjoyed the contest.

Tornadoes spun around the cluster of beasts forcing some to huddle against the wind. Others stretched their claws against the invisible enemy.

The demons roared away, having again met their match after so many years.

Keja brushed his still-watering eyes. "Is it over?" he asked.

"For tonight," the shaggy beast answered, smiling broadly. "I think they enjoyed that. They must not get adequate opposition from the skeleton men."

The battle with the wind demons had lasted only a short while, but Keja sent Djinn to check the Skeleton Lord's chambers once more.

Giles watched the Skeleton Lord pacing back and forth, muttering, lifting a beaker now and again to sniff at it. "Why is the blood so important?" he asked.

The Skeleton Lord peered at him over the beakers and flasks. "It's the fluid of life, of power."

"But it's only useful inside a body. Once it has drained away, there is no life force, no power. I've fought against men who thought it contained the strength and cunning of their enemies and who drank it after battle." Giles chuckled. "We defeated them in battle time and again. The blood did them no good."

The Skeleton Lord glared at Giles. "No, another reason. Their gods abandoned them, they were outnumbered. Some other cause. Blood is powerful, even animal blood. In the desert there are great cats, strong and wily." He lifted a flask and held it toward Giles. "See. This is blood from one of them. I will find the essence of those qualities in their blood. Then my skeleton men will be more powerful, more deceptive!"

He gestured at the array of equipment on the tables. "All my labors are toward better warriors and leaders, not followers like these slow-wits."

"You can't give men what they don't already have," Giles said. "If they are not courageous, not leaders, can't think for themselves, no amount of blood from human or animal will change them. I once saw a hunter who killed a deer. When he butchered it, he pulled out its heart and ate it raw. He said it gave him great skill in the forest, the same skill as the deer once possessed. I told him that the deer did not have any great skill or it would not have been killed. The hunter got angry at that."

"The hunter was right," the Skeleton Lord said. "You are wrong."

"So he told me. He tried to force me to eat part of the heart. I fought him and he lost. I buried the remains of the heart in the grave with him and went away."

"But a deer is not strong," the Lord replied. "It lives by its wits. It lies low during the day, feeds only in the morning and evening, is afraid of its enemies. It runs from danger. Deer are cowardly animals."

"Not cowardly—cautious. Have you ever seen stags fighting during rutting time? You cannot call them cowardly. They fight to the death."

The Skeleton Lord made an obscene gesture. "That is what the animal will do for sex," he said, dismissing Giles' argument.

"Humans are no better, then," Giles replied with a smile. "Sex is a strong drive, but your skeleton men don't have that drive any longer. You took it away from them, is that not so?"

"They do not need it. There are no women here."

"Give your warriors back their sex and allow them to have wives, concubines, lovers. You will have stronger soldiers. They will have something to fight for."

"No!" An anguished roar came from the Skeleton Lord,

his voice no longer reedy. "They need fight only for *me*!"

A commotion in the outer chamber interrupted them. The heavy tread of skeleton men was nearly obscured by Anji's sharp voice shouting, "No, no."

Guards held the boy's arms on either side, almost lifting him off his feet.

The Skeleton Lord stared thoughtfully at Anji. "Put him down. He can do no harm." He waved his hand at the guards. "You're dismissed."

The Lord rubbed his hands together and looked at Giles. "One of your party, I see. We'll have them all before long. You'll be no farther on your quest than when you were locked in the dungeon. And, you, young one, where have you been these past hours?"

Anji looked at the Skeleton Lord and then to Giles. "I was just trying to help. We thought we could find . . . it."

Flinging himself at Giles, he threw his arms around the man's neck and wept. Giles murmured, "It's all right. It will be all right."

"You have affection for the boy?" The Skeleton Lord looked bemused, as if this were an entirely new idea. He bent forward to examine the boy more closely, expecting to find some quality that caused the emotion in Giles. "Amazing," he muttered. "Looks like an ordinary Trans to me."

He called to his guards. They pulled Anji away from Giles, twisting his arms behind him. "Put him over in the corner," the Skeleton Lord said.

"There's no need to be rough on the boy," Giles said.

"He means that much to you?" the Skeleton Lord asked. "Perhaps we can bargain. You'd like me to turn the boy loose, wouldn't you?"

"He can't do any harm. Let him go. He's only a youngster."

"If you tell the others to surrender and take my guards to their hiding place, then I think it could be arranged."

"And what would you do with him? Cast him out into the desert to die?"

The Skeleton Lord laughed. "You have no trust, warrior. No trust. We would take him to meet the caravan to Kasha. He would be safe."

Giles wondered if he could trust the insane man. Keja would certainly be angry with him, but the boy had to be freed. Giles felt a hundred years older and tireder in that instant—all the more reason for him to make the decision. Anji deserved the chance to grow up and live his own life.

"I'll tell you where they are and convince them to surrender if you guarantee the boy will be treated well and taken to the caravan."

The Skeleton Lord threw back his head and laughed so hard that he choked. When he had caught his breath again, he wiped his eyes and shook his head at Giles. "What a fool you are. You have no power to bargain. You sit there, like some wild pig in a pen, talking as if we were merchants signing a contract. You have no wealth, no army, no power. You are nothing."

The Lord waved his arms and stomped back and forth in front of Giles. "You think I am mad. You and the boy are merely midges flying busily about, thinking to disturb my great work. And your companions are gnats." He gestured to the tables where his experiments bubbled.

"I'll have the boy's blood for my work. It will bubble merrily, don't you think? Perhaps it is younger blood that I need. A perfect opportunity to find out."

"The boy's blood will do you no good," Giles said. "You're looking for strength, courage, decisiveness, the qualities that will make a stronger soldier. You won't find those things in a boy his age. He's had no experiences yet to gain the characteristics you seek." Giles spat. "Foolish, a waste of time. I have had those experiences. If you must, take my blood.

"Twenty years at war," he boasted. "Leading men, killing my enemies, crazy with the smell of battle, wading in when we were outnumbered. That is the blood you want. A more than fair trade for the boy."

The Skeleton Lord perched upon a stool as he watched a simmering solution. Giles knew that he was considering the offer.

"You have a point," the Lord said. "But I have both of you. Why not experiment on *both* your bloods?" The cackle chilled Giles to the core of his being.

* * *

Petia hunted but had seen nothing of Anji or Sleek. A short while back she had felt an empathic tug that told her Anji was in trouble, but she had no idea on which level to look.

Earlier she had paused at the end of one corridor, frightened by a loud roaring. It sounded like a storm blowing through a nearby corridor. Before she could investigate, the sound disappeared.

She crept to the corner and stretched out along the floor. Edging forward slowly, she could look down the adjoining hall. Sleek backed toward her.

"Sleek," she whispered. The young female beast leaped and twisted, eyes wide with fear. She let out her pent-up breath when she recognized Petia.

"Where's Anji?" Petia asked. "Wasn't he with you?"

"He was, but we got separated. I don't know where he is." The young beast was desolate.

"He's been captured," Petia said. "I feel it. What did you two think you were doing?"

Sleek's eyes filled with tears. "He said he could find this key you seek. I just wanted to prove that not all us beasts are cowards like Giles said."

"Don't worry about it now. We've got to find Anji. If he's been captured, he'd be taken to the Skeleton Lord's chambers."

Sleek shivered, but Petia put a hand on her shoulder and squeezed, showing her confidence in the beast. The two set off silently down the hall.

"Djinn?" Keja fumed, standing with one foot on the top step, waiting for the djinn to return. "Where is he? It shouldn't take that long."

"Patience," Red Mane said. "Or are you in a hurry to do battle? Giles would tell you that if there is a possibility of knowing your enemy's strength, it would be best to wait and find that out."

"You're right," Keja muttered, not liking it when the beast was right and he was wrong. He didn't know where any of his companions were, and it wouldn't help them to rush into a trap. If they had been captured, he would rescue them.

"Djinn?"

"I'm back."

The voice whispered in Keja's ear, and he jumped. "Djinn! What did you find?"

"Giles is there. Anji, too, but neither one is tied. They're being held at spear point. They don't think Anji is any threat to them."

"How many guards are there?"

"Five in the chambers," Djinn replied. "Eight outside in the corridor. We outnumber them."

"We must be careful. Even if we capture the Skeleton Lord, we don't know how many troops are scattered around this city, or what they'll do." He turned to the beasts behind him. "Everybody ready?"

"Wait, Keja, there's more. I heard a noise in another corridor and found Petia and Sleek."

"Where? Can you stay visible long enough to lead us to them?"

"Down this corridor and around the corner. Follow me."

"There's no sense for all of us to go there and then come back. Just this once, stay visible. Go get them and bring them here. Can you do that?"

Djinn winked and was gone. In a few minutes he returned with Petia and Sleek in tow.

Keja started in on Petia immediately. "What made you go off like that? Giles went looking for you and now he's captured. Anji's captured, too."

Her eyes flashed. "I had to go look for the boy. I'm the only one who cares about him."

Red Mane growled deep in his throat. The two stopped and looked at him. "You can argue all you want when this is done. We must hurry if we are going to get on with it."

"You're right," Keja said. "Djinn, where are you now? Fade away now; you can be more useful if they can't see you." Keja turned to the Trans woman. "We're going to attack the chambers and release Giles and Anji. Keep your weapons loose."

Djinn faded in again. "I've checked again. There are more guards in the hall now, reinforcements."

"We'll have to fight our way in. I don't think we can plan any further than a battle in the passageway. After that, we'll do whatever we can. I still think we can win, even if we are outnumbered."

He lifted his hand and motioned the beasts forward. They moved toward the final passageway that held the Skeleton Lord's chambers and death.

Chapter Sixteen

"A warrior's blood, yes. And a young boy's blood, too." The Skeleton Lord cackled. "I will have both. It will be an interesting experiment. The alchemy of youth and courage might be the answer."

"Damn your lying eyes," Giles shouted. "You promised to exchange the boy for me. You said he could go free."

The Skeleton Lord's eyes narrowed to dagger points, threatening to pierce Giles' very soul. "Who are you to bargain with me? A vagabond appearing out of the desert. I am the power here. You are so much sand, blowing into cracks and crevices. Nothing, you are nothing!" His voice rose to a scream with his final words.

"Guards, bring him to my work table. No, you idiots, the big one."

Giles struggled ineffectually against the skeleton men. The Lord held a short blade in his hands. He stropped it on a leather strap. "I'll take only a little now, but I'll keep you around, taking a few drops more each time."

The Skeleton Lord steadied Giles' arm, turning the wrist to expose the veins. Touching the spot where Giles' exertions had caused the vessels to stand out, he carefully lowered his knife.

"Now," Keja shouted. Ahead he saw skeleton men standing at ease before the Lord's chamber door. Four of them turned toward the advancing beast throng, and there were at least a dozen more standing farther down the hall.

Red Mane threw back his head and roared and the other beasts took up the call. The guards hesitated for a brief instant. It was to give the attackers a small advantage. Keja raised his sword to slash, picked out a target and ran faster.

The leading skeleton warrior attempted to back away

from Keja so that he could use his spear. Other guards crowded behind. He reached deliberately for a short dagger at his hip.

Keja raised his sword waist high. Gripping the edge of the sword below the hilt with his left hand, he drove the blade with both hands into the guard's ribcage, smashing bones and destroying the warrior. Keja stepped back, pulled the weapon loose and watched the guard rattle to the floor.

Petia and Sleek attacked side by side. Petia slashed hard with her short sword aiming for her opponent's eyes. As the guard retreated, Sleek rushed in, clawing at unprotected legs.

Red Mane became a fury, roaring encouragement to the other beasts. He burst through the first line of guards and attacked the guards farther along the hall. Several beasts followed him through the break, one beast leaping five feet onto the chest of a guard, taking him and several others down to the ground. With savage fangs, he broke exposed bones and left the skeleton warriors helpless.

Giles heard the fighting outside and struggled harder against the hands holding his wrist steady for the Skeleton Lord's knife.

"They want their city back," he shouted, "and I don't think either you or your guards will keep them from it."

The blade trembled in the Skeleton Lord's hand. "Leaal!" he screamed.

Giles had forgotten the advisor and looked for the man. He did not see him and dismissed him. Giles, himself, yelled, "Djinn!"

The blade flashed down and slashed Giles' wrist. He looked at the Skeleton Lord, surprised at his presence of mind. The sounds of the fierce fighting echoed from the corridor. The Skeleton Lord bent over, intent on licking the blood that dripped from Giles' wrist.

Giles brought his knee up and caught the Skeleton Lord in the groin; Giles grimaced when he felt little more than bone, but the Lord rocked back against the table, gasping for breath.

"Djinn!" Giles shouted again.

Keja appeared at the doorway and diverted the guards'

attention. Giles ripped free of their grasp. He swung his fist
at the Skeleton Lord's face.

Djinn finally appeared, smiling. "You called?" he asked
pleasantly, as if the carnage around him meant nothing.

"You took your time," Giles snarled. "Destroy everything on the tables."

Djinn grinned wickedly. The glassware was a symbol of
all that he had suffered. He thrust out one muscular arm
and swept down one side of the table. Glassware clattered
over the end and smashed onto the stone floor. He turned
down the aisle between the two tables, an arm on either side
sweeping beakers, vials and other containers before him.
Reeking pools of liquids and glass spattered the floor.

The Skeleton Lord stood transfixed as the glassware
clattered along his worktables. He saw his creations being
destroyed: chemicals, tinctures, amalgams and bloods
mixed haphazardly atop the smooth alabaster work surface.
He sagged.

Snatching up a sword, Giles went to assist the others. He
saw the strength ebbed out of the Skeleton Lord; he was
defeated. A fierce cry behind Giles startled him. The
sorcerer threw back his head. His back arched as he
screamed, "Leaal!"

Petia glanced up from the skeleton man she had killed.
Rounding the end of the corridor she saw the Lord's advisor
running pell-mell, gesturing to the guards behind him.
"Hurry, you fools. Kill them. Kill them all!" he screamed.
The guards broke into a travesty of a run, their feet
pounding flatly on the stone.

"Red Mane," she shouted. "Reinforcements." The shaggy beast motioned to those not occupied in fighting. Red
Mane's eyes gleamed as they fastened on the advisor.

Red Mane struck Leaal across the face, and the advisor
sank to the floor. A second slash left him bleeding and
already dying. For a moment Red Mane felt pleasure in his
revenge, then pity. He glanced up, seeking another opponent. There was none. The skeleton men stumbled down
the hall away from them. "After them," Red Mane shouted.

"No," Petia yelled. Emphatically she knew the skeleton
men were beaten, confused. Without a leader, they were
like lost children. "Capture them later."

In the Lord's chamber, liquids dripped onto the floor, a thin spiral of smoke floating upward from one such mixture. Flame leaped upward and spread rapidly across the chamber to lick at the fringe of tapestries hanging on the walls.

Giles felt the heat at his back. He swung at the skeleton man before him, forcing him back. He turned to find sheets of flame already covering two walls. An ominous thought ran through his mind.

The key might be hidden here! He snatched at a burning tapestry, tearing it from the wall and flinging it to the floor. It landed in a pool of liquid and he stamped on it, trying to put the fire out. Flame shot up his leg. He leaped away, grabbed a cloak from a hook and attempted to beat out the fire.

The Skeleton Lord's volatile reagents spread the fire despite Giles' efforts; the wooden legs of the alabaster tables burned like kindling. One table crashed, spilling more liquid to the floor. Liquid and flame raced across the floor, moving to the outer room.

The fire spread. How hot must it be before gold melted? he wondered. Their quest might well end in this blazing room.

He heard a muttering behind him and turned to find the Skeleton Lord staggering toward him, hands outstretched. One bony finger pointed at Giles and the reedy voice rose, mouthing a spell. The language was not familiar to Giles, but the spell's impact shook him. A tingling ran through Giles' chest; his arms felt leaden, as if he had been lifting hundredweights of flour; he couldn't move his feet.

Djinn entered the blazing outer chamber beside Keja. He gasped in Keja's ear, "It's a spell to freeze Giles. Don't let him finish it."

Keja dashed across the room and caught the Skeleton Lord's arm, twisting it behind him. The sorcerer yelled in pain, and Keja clamped a hand over his mouth.

"Some rags, anything to stuff in his mouth." Djinn floated toward him with several scarves he snatched from a shelf. Keja shoved two of them into the Skeleton Lord's mouth.

Rushing to Giles, he asked, "Are you all right?"

Giles rubbed his arms and stamped his legs. "Thanks," he said. "A few more words and he would have had me. A powerful spell. I'm glad you got here in time."

"I saw him use that spell before," Djinn said. "It would have frozen you like a statue."

Petia cried out from the corridor. "More guards; human, I think. Not skeleton men. And the beasts are gone."

Keja and Djinn headed for the doorway. Giles paused to look for his magical sword but couldn't find it. He hated to lose it, but he had little time for further searching. He kicked at a burning spot and swore, then realized that Anji stood by his side. He shoved the boy ahead of him. "Don't you have any sense at all? Stay out of the way."

Giles looked frantically for his sword until the heat drove him from the chamber. He pulled a spear from the hands of a dead skeleton man and reluctantly joined his companions. Out in the corridor men rushed toward them. As they drew closer, he recognized them as Harifim, the desert tribesmen. He had experienced their ferocity in Kasha. Now he would try to even the score.

Keja, Petia and Giles ranged themselves across the hallway, on the defensive. They fought well, but the Harifim forced them back with a fierce attack. Giles found the spear a clumsy weapon. He could do little more than defend himself.

Petia heard a cry from inside the chamber. "Anji," she yelled and drove two opponents back with a maniacal attack. She reached the doorway and leaped inside, leaving Giles and Keja to fight on.

Anji stood, his arms loaded with bound volumes from the sorcerer's shelves. The Skeleton Lord, his body on fire, burned like tinder. Petia watched as the body wrenched once, twice, then fell limp. What life had been in the demented mind and twisted soul ended in fire. Flames fully enveloped the room. Petia thrust the boy behind her.

"We've got to get out or we'll suffocate," she yelled. "Follow me."

Petia halted at the doorway. The beasts had returned and were attacking the Harifim from the rear, giving Giles and Keja the chance to take the offensive. Harifim began dying; others fought on, but the attack of the beasts had taken the fight out of them. One gestured with his free hand and laid down his sword. Giles and Keja drew back, waiting to see what the others would do. The fight ended. Seven men surrendered, two were wounded, two lay dead.

"Djinn, find something to bind them with." Giles kicked the swords across the corridor. "Is everyone accounted for?" He counted his own party and caught Red Mane's nod.

He ran back into the blazing room. Petia called after him that the Skeleton Lord was dead, but he didn't hear her.

The Lord's blackened bones sprawled on the floor. The desiccated flesh had burned completely. The Skeleton Lord was not only dead, but truly a skeleton. Shielding his eyes with one arm, Giles tried vainly to find his sword. Smoke billowed and hung thickly in the room. A shelf clattered to the floor, spilling charts and showering sparks. Intense heat forced him back. Rivulets of sweat stung his eyes. When he couldn't hold his breath any longer, he stumbled from the room.

In the hallway, he sucked in great drafts of fresh air. Petia wiped his face. "I yelled at you that he was dead. Didn't you hear me?"

"My sword—I couldn't find it," he gasped. A blinding flash illumined the room, reflecting off the corridor walls. "I think that was it. The end of a wonderful weapon."

Giles straightened. "Djinn, put these men in the dungeon. Let them carry their own wounded. Then accompany Red Mane and the beasts and search the entire city. Round up any skeleton men. See that our old friend Teloq locks them in the cages."

"I'm starved, Giles," Keja said. "Couldn't Djinn find something for us to eat first? If there are men here"—he gestured at the Harifim—"there must be food, a pantry, something. And something to drink. By the gods, even water will do."

"All right. That first, Djinn. Then we'll round up any who are left."

Djinn herded the Harifim down the passage, followed by two beasts who Red Mane had singled out. He wanted to be sure that these ancient enemies had no opportunity for further mischief. When the men had been locked in an empty room, the beasts returned. Djinn drifted away and disappeared down a stairway.

"Let's get away from the smoke," Petia suggested. "The city can't catch fire. It's solid rock. When the furnishings have burned, the fire will go out."

Giles peered through the doorway. Nothing could be retrieved now. Everything flammable was burning. Smoke and scorch marks covered the white walls. He nodded. "Good idea. Let's go where we can breathe fresh air."

The company trooped down one level and collapsed along the walls. For a long time no one spoke. Sighs of contentment came from the beasts. They had proven themselves, and the city was theirs once more.

Giles reached over and tousled Anji's hair. The boy leaned on one elbow on the stack of books he had rescued from the Skeleton Lord's shelves. "You're the only one with any sense," Giles said. "We promised Djinn that we'd try to change him back to a human. Without those books, we wouldn't have had a chance. I hope you grabbed the right ones."

Anji grinned. "Are you glad that I came along? I'm good for some things. I'm good with the *lirjan*. But I didn't find your key and sometimes I get in the way, don't I?"

Giles smiled and nodded. He had probably been in someone's way when he was eleven, too. That was an ancient time for him, beyond remembrance. The faces of his own parents blurred with the years. Even the memory of his wife, Leorra, and his sons dimmed. Too tired. He'd try again this evening when he went to sleep. Maybe he'd dream of them.

"I've found the pantry and kitchen," Djinn announced. "There's plenty of food. Follow me."

Plain food, washed down with a fruity wine, raised the spirits of the company. With stomachs full, they wanted nothing more than a nap, but Red Mane and Giles roused them. They swept the city in an organized manner. Djinn ferreted out the hiding Harifim and skeleton men. The older beasts delighted in finding long-forgotten passageways and rooms, many of which were closed. Parts of Shahal had not been used for decades.

Giles climbed wearily to the top level. The Skeleton

Lord's chambers were scorched ruins. Ash swirled in the evening breezes. Perhaps the *pazuzi* would swirl it all away during their nightly forays. He had little hope of finding sword or key, Giles thought grimly, but tomorrow they would search.

The key to the Gate of Paradise might not have been destroyed. But tonight he wanted only to sleep.

Chapter Seventeen

The odor of death still hung in the Skeleton Lord's rooms, but it no longer overpowered them. Petia rolled up the sleeves of her robe to begin sifting through the debris for the key to the Gate of Paradise. "What do you want us to do, Giles?"

He stared at the piles of ash-covered rubbish. Molten glass adhered to the floor in the inner chamber. Charred paper and portions of books lay at one edge of the outer room. He picked up a small piece of metal, its twisted shape testifying to the fire's immense heat. Relief replaced worry; for a heart-wrenching moment he thought it might have once been a key.

The key.

He threw it down in disgust. "We've got to sift through this stuff. There are only two things that I'm looking for. One is the key, although I'm afraid that if it were here, it would be as twisted as that piece of brass. The other is my sword. I don't have much hope for it, either."

Giles, Petia and Keja set about the task, plunging their arms into the mess, moving methodically from one side of the room to the other. They found several metal objects, but none of gold.

It took an hour to sift through the detritus of the outer room. When they reached the inner chamber, Giles hurried on. "This is where the sword should be, or what's left of it." He scrabbled through the ashes to the side of the room where he had lain trussed the evening before. "Ah," he said. "I can feel the hilt." He tugged and his hand came away with the twisted pommel, hilt and crossbar of the sword —but no blade.

Disappointment clouded his face. "So much for that wonderful sword. I suspected this last night when I saw the

172

light flash. Whatever magicks were contained within its steel were released in one quick lightning bolt."

Searching the rest of the chamber took much less time. They searched carefully but found nothing but molten glass, stained by the substances they had once contained. Keja and Giles struggled to move the alabaster tables but found nothing beneath them.

"I'm sure that the key wasn't in these rooms," Giles said. "It'll turn up somewhere else. Let's go clean up and see if there is any ale in the pantry. We deserve it." He tried to sound cheerful, but Petia knew that he was disconsolate about the sword.

Over cheese and ale, Petia said dreamily, "It might be worth our while to stay here for a few months. We could help the beasts make plans for restoring the city and take our time searching for the key. And," she added in a lower voice, "lead a more normal life."

"First we've got to do something with all the prisoners we've taken," Giles said. "We can't keep them locked up forever. They'll starve."

"No loss," said Keja, stuffing a large hunk of coarse bread into his mouth and washing it down with a healthy swig of ale.

Sleek and some of the other beasts entered the room, grinning. They had been ranging up and down the levels, rediscovering their city.

"Glad to see someone's happy," Giles said. "Is Shahal all you expected it to be?"

"Yes, dirty and dusty from neglect, but we'll soon set that right," Sleek said. The other beasts chorused their pleasure with the rock city. "Red Mane will be here soon. He's climbed several levels higher to look out over the desert. He wanted to be alone, but I don't think he wants us to see how pleased he is to be home again."

"Bring us a couple of the skeleton men," Giles asked the beasts. "We're going to have to do something with them sooner or later. It might as well be done now." Torn Ear and several of the younger beasts trotted off to comply.

The two skeleton men they brought stared into space, sunken eyesockets showing no emotion. Giles forced himself to peer closer at them. There *were* eyes there—they had just become minuscule through the Skeleton Lord's magicks. Giles ran his hand down the man's arm. "Bony, but there is still some flesh there," he observed. He put his hand to the man's hollow chest and was surprised to feel a regular heart beat, even though he saw nothing in the cavity.

He peered into the man's almost-invisible eyes. They stared, trancelike and didn't focus on Giles or follow him when he moved. He waved his hand in front of the skeleton man's face. No reaction. He pushed one man ahead of him across the floor, receiving no resistance. "It's almost as if they were drugged."

"Definitely a spell," Petia said. "Ever since I've been trying to tap into the emotions of others, I've felt the use of magic around me. Not much, maybe not enough to be useful, but I've sensed it. These men are not permanently changed," she finished with finality.

"Do you think you can touch them emotionally?" Giles asked. He saw Petia's distaste at the idea. But she had another idea.

"I'm no sorcerer, but what about the books Anji rescued? Maybe I can use some of my skill to make them humans again." Petia didn't speak with great conviction, but Giles saw that she was willing to try. He motioned to a young beast, who brought the rescued grimoires to the table.

Petia turned the spines of the stack toward her. Alchemical symbols of unknown meaning adorned each spine. She pulled the top book to her and opened the cover, hoping to find a clue to the contents.

There was none. Sighing, she settled in for a long search. "Giles, you can read. Go through another volume. A binding spell might have the counterspell added on to the end."

Together they pored over page after dusty page. Petia found some pages in strange, unreadable languages. As the morning wore on, the two lost themselves in the fascination of what they could read in the books. Occasionally Petia shuddered and hurriedly turned the page. "There's some unsavory work in here," she muttered.

"I've noticed," Giles replied.

He was ready to suggest a break when Petia exclaimed, "I've found it!"

Giles read over her shoulder. When he finished, he asked, "Are you willing to try it?"

"I guess I'm ready." She sounded uncertain.

He brought a skeleton man to stand in front of her. She lifted the book and read the words aloud, speaking slowly, pausing to watch for any reaction. When she had finished the spell, she set the book down. For long seconds there was no response. Giles grabbed the man when he began to shiver, as if his bones had caught cold. Then Giles pulled away—flesh formed under his very fingers. The man's eyes grew to human proportion, cleared and focused. Facial skin and flesh puffed up to give definition to the angularity of his bony structure. Faster and faster the transformation ran until a swarthy, normal-looking human stood before them, bewildered.

He turned his head and looked about him, obviously confused.

"Do you know where you are?" Petia asked.

"No." The word came like a key turning in a rusty lock.

"Does Shahal mean anything to you? Or the Skeleton Lord?"

"I remember being captured in the desert. By magic! There were fourteen of my clan with me. We were brought to the rock. There was a man called the Skeleton Lord. Yes, that I remember—but nothing more."

He looked around the room and tensed defensively when he saw the beasts. He pointed a finger at them and said, "Don't let them harm me!"

"Are you afraid of them?" Giles asked quietly.

"Yes, they are powerful. They roam the desert. We . . ." He paused, as if a new thought had come to him. "We leave them alone."

"Who is 'we'?" Giles prodded.

"The Harifim, the people of the desert."

Red Mane walked over and stood in front of the man. "Do you remember when this city, Shahal, was on the trade route?" The man did not. "So much has been lost." Red Mane sighed gustily.

"What do you mean?" Giles asked.

"Masser is an important port and trade center on Bandanarra's eastern coast. Galhib was an inland center, a transfer point for caravans between Kasha and Kuilla. Shahal is halfway between Galhib and Masser, on the Track of Fourteen. The route was so called because it took fourteen days to travel from Galhib to Masser. All the caravans stopped here for a day's rest." Red Mane straightened. "Perhaps we can make it so again. We have to try."

Giles recognized the despair in Red Mane's voice. He would encourage the beasts as much as possible, but there was much left to do.

"There are stories in my clan," the former skeleton man said, "that we were once wealthy and traded throughout the desert. But that was long before my memory."

"It can be so again," Giles said. "If you will work together with the beasts of Shahal." He turned to Petia. "Try the other one."

Petia read the spell more easily this time; the second skeleton man regained his bodily contours and looked around him apprehensively. Giles examined both of the men. They appeared to be in good health, although thinner than any of the tough desert men he had seen. Regular meals would change that, he was convinced.

Keja entered the room. "I can't believe this place. It's incredible. The Skeleton Lord ruined a perfectly fine city, but that'll change soon enough." His enthusiasm blazed through the room.

While Giles elicited the aid of the two freed Harifim, Petia tried to release two skeleton men with one reading but found that it did not work. "I hope there aren't too many of them," she said as she prepared to begin again.

"The Skeleton Lord had many of them. I'm surprised that there are any Harifim left in the desert. It seems as if they are all in Shahal."

Red Mane came over to where Giles and the two Harifim spoke quietly. The beast obviously steeled himself for what he had to say. "We have agreed to share in the profits from trade if we can sign a treaty with the Harifim leaders. We can send these two back as emissaries to show our good intentions. Too many have suffered at the Lord's hand. We must work together to regain all we lost so long ago."

"Excellent," Giles said. "Have you thought about the Calabrashio Seas? You're going to have to find another route."

"We'll find one. One step at a time."

As Petia released the skeleton men one by one, the room became crowded, and she grew weary during the afternoon. She rested briefly and Giles hovered over her, making sure that she took some hot broth. She had memorized the spell and spoke it easily now, but each repetition took a bit more out of her. By the time she had finished, she collapsed in exhaustion.

During the evening, Petia sat quietly while the others discussed the day's events. Anji found a brush and sat running it through Petia's hair, draining away her tensions. Occasionally her eyes closed and she nodded, but she forced herself awake to listen to the conversation. Even though tired, she caught snippets of emotion rolling through the room like waves against a sandy shore.

"We have to begin searching for the key," Keja said. "I don't intend to spend all my time feeding the prisoners and making sure they don't turn on us."

"We won't spend all our time on them," Giles said. "Today was different, erasing the spells. Beginning tomorrow, we will search."

Red Mane spoke up. "We'll all help. We owe it to you." Giles started to protest, but Red Mane stopped him. "You have helped us to regain our city. We will help you. If Djinn were here he could lend his assistance, too."

Djinn slowly materialized at Giles' elbow. He scowled and crossed his massive arms.

"What's the matter with you?" Giles asked.

"Petia has loosed all the skeleton men. What about our bargain? You said you'd change me back into human form." He glowered at them.

"If you'd stay in plain sight we wouldn't forget you so easily," Giles remonstrated. "Petia, loose this fellow so he gets that ugly frown off his face. I'll bet he's good-looking when he's in a better humor."

Petia stirred. She knew the loosing spell by heart. She recited the words slowly, looking at Djinn and wondering what transformation he would go through. When she finished the unbinding magicks, she stood back, waiting.

Djinn floated several inches off the floor. He watched Petia as she said the words, then looked down at his body, waiting for the changes. Nothing happened.

He frowned. "I feel the same."

"I'm sorry, Djinn," Petia said. "I'm so tired, I must have forgotten some of the words. Let me get the book."

Anji ran to the table and came back with the grimoire. Petia opened it to the proper page and intoned the loosing spell carefully, looking at each word as she said it aloud. When she had finished she closed the book and waited. Again there was no change in the djinn. Stunned, Petia stared from the book to Djinn and back.

"You promised . . ." Djinn began, vaporous tears forming in the corner of his eyes.

"I know we did, Djinn." Petia reached out to him. "It must be a different spell. I'll try tomorrow; I'm exhausted tonight. But I'll find it, I promise I will." She realized that she spoke to empty air. He had disappeared.

"It's not fair," she said. "He's given us so much help, while the skeleton men were our enemies. They've been released, and he's still a captive of the Lord's magicks."

Giles put his hand on Petia's shoulder. "Get some sleep. Tomorrow when you're fresh, you'll have a clear head to find the proper spell."

She nodded. "If it's here. I don't think I can face Djinn if it's not." She rose wearily and, leaning on Anji, left the room.

In the morning, Petia leafed through the books, looking for a spell to release Djinn. She found neither a spell for turning a human into a djinn, nor for releasing one. Giles sat on one side of her and Keja on the other, helping in the search. They found nothing.

"What are we going to do?" Petia asked.

"We're going to search for the key," Giles replied. "This evening we'll go over the spell book again. Try not to think about it during the day. We'll come to it with fresh minds this evening."

The beasts helped make the search much easier. Giles described the size and shape of the key and told them that it was crafted of gold. The beasts understood and knew the kind of places it might be hidden. They worked in pairs and started at the lowest level of the city.

When they stopped for the midday meal, they had explored the first six floors. Their spirits were high and they wagered good-naturedly on who would be the one to find the key.

Petia took her cup of tea to a separate table and leafed through the spell books once again. In spite of what Giles had said, her inability to release Djinn preyed on her mind. She studied the pages more carefully until it was time to take up the search for the Key to Paradise once again.

The seventh floor brought memories of the battle with the Skeleton Lord. Having searched the Lord's chambers, they concentrated on the other rooms. They found nothing and moved on to the upper floors.

By late afternoon Giles wondered if he should call off the search. Fatigue might cause them to miss an important clue. Yet they were nearing the top of Shahal and he was anxious. If they did not find the key, they must begin again and search more carefully.

He walked to the end of an open corridor and leaned against the balustrade, staring out over the desert. The sun was sinking and he shielded his eyes from the red glare. Dry and desolate as the terrain was, it held its own beauty.

Gleaming rock cliffs stood like fortresses at the edge of the plain. Streaks of color cascaded down their faces. Giles caught the scent of water wafted from some distant oasis. He would be happy to leave, but he was not displeased that he had been here. After all, had he not wanted to explore the world and wash away the tastes of war? To give purpose once again to a life that had turned into pointless drifting? He had explored more of the world than most. Joining company with those two rogues, Keja and Petia, had led him far from the place of his birth—but that wasn't home. Home no longer existed for him. Maybe it didn't matter whether they found the key or not. Being with good companions held its own reward.

"Giles, come quickly."

He turned toward Petia and, tired, ambled toward the excitement at the end of the corridor. Nothing, not even the key, could make him hurry.

Petia bounced up and down. "She's found it. Sleek's found it."

"Where?"

"Down here. Follow me."

Giles paused at the threshold to a room that had been sealed shut and hidden by clever plastering. Was it really over? He stepped into the room and stood transfixed. On the far side stood a huge throne, its arms and high back decorated with strangely unsettling symbols. Seated on it was the chalky white skeleton of a giant. Giles swallowed hard. It looked as if some ancient king had seated himself and died, left foot forward, right elbow resting on the throne's arm, skull tipped forward and eyeless sockets studying something in his lap.

Giles followed the gaze. In one outstretched skeletal hand rested a gold key. In the other was a scroll.

"Aren't you going to pick it up?" Petia asked eagerly.

Giles almost reverently advanced to the throne. The others crowded behind him. He picked up the key and examined it briefly. "This is it," he said, holding it aloft. He handed it to Petia, and the key made the rounds of the people and beasts in the room.

Slowly, Giles unrolled the scroll. The map drawn on it was a work of art. Lettering of exquisite calligraphy decorated the upper left-hand corner and told of the Gate of Paradise. The body of the scroll portrayed an unknown country with mountains, forests and the sea coast, all colored in delicate paints. In the lower right-hand corner a key was depicted in gold leaf. The key's shank was set with a green gemstone, apparently an emerald. Large, ornate letters sprawled across the main body of the map: KHELORA.

"The location of the final key," Giles said, his voice hardly more than a husky whisper.

Chapter Eighteen

"We'll stay for a while and help you get started," Giles said. "It's only fair since you found the key for us."

"You don't have to stay," Red Mane said. "We're grateful to you, also. We've derived more benefit than you have, to my way of thinking. We have regained our city—and our self-esteem."

Giles laughed. "If we keep congratulating each other, nothing will get done. Now, it seems to me that this wing will provide the immediate housing you need, with easy access to the pantry, scullery and dining hall." Soon they were engrossed in the plans.

Keja sat, bemused at the evening's activities. He felt left out, as usual, but he had much to ponder. They would be leaving soon, and they no longer had any animals. The *lirjan* would have wandered away. Supplies were needed. Those problems would have to be resolved.

And the keys. He thought of the keys. Four of them now. One more to go.

He leaned back, hands laced behind his head, and watched Petia with Anji. She had gone domestic, at least in the quiet moments. She could still fight right alongside himself and Giles, but the boy had brought a change to her. Still, she looked lovely. Her cat features only heightened her beauty, lending an exotic quality to her. Keja tried to sort out what he really felt for her. He failed.

Yawning, he went to his bedroll, still mulling over the key, Petia, Giles, and what might be in store for them in Khelora. His dreams were of the final key, the Gate of Paradise, what he would find behind the Gate—and intermixed with it ran a frolicking, smiling Petia.

The following morning, Keja went to Giles with his

concern about pack animals for their journey. With Red
Mane they interviewed the Harifim and selected two to
carry the offer of truce back to their people. The beasts
hoped this would be the beginning of negotiations with the
people of all desert tribes.

Giles and Keja hoped that the men would return with
lirjan or horses they could buy. They watched the recovered
skeleton men set off across the desert plain and returned to
the work at hand.

"Take whatever you wish from the treasure room. You
will need money for passage home," Red Mane offered.

"You are too generous," Giles said. Rather than hunting
for gold, he took the opportunity to search for a new sword.
He regretted the loss of the sword of power. Eventually he
found a serviceable sword, but one which he'd replace at
the first opportunity. He left the choosing of jewels and
coinage to Petia, Keja and Anji.

Surrounded by immense wealth in the treasure room,
they played with the fortune, running ropes of pearls
through their fingers, scooping up gold and silver coins and
flinging them into the air, whooping with delight as they
jangled together.

"It's funny," Petia said. "We seek out the five keys that
will give us untold wealth, and here we sit, like children. We
could take enough to keep us comfortably for the rest of our
lives and forget about the last key."

Keja whooped. "We're all mad." In the end, however,
they took only a modest amount, this being all they might
safely carry across the desert.

"The beasts will need it to begin trade again," Petia said.
She gazed wistfully at the ruby brooch in her hand, then
placed it gently back on the pile. "Let's get out of here. It's
depressing to think of leaving anything."

Keja laughed. "What is even more depressing is that Red
Mane is *giving* all this to us. There's no challenge. I wish I
could *steal* it!"

Petia continued her search through the spell books. She
turned every leaf and studied the many volumes Anji had
rescued but to no avail. She found nothing about turning a
human into a djinn, or a djinn into a human.

Djinn remained invisible, angry. Petia ached for him.

She knew how he must feel, watching the skeleton men regain their humanity, beginning to put on weight and looking normal again. They had been the enemy.

She opened the cover of a book and began again. If it were not possible to change Djinn, it would be no fault of hers. She pushed her hair back from her eyes with quick, catlike preening gestures and settled to the task. Anji stood at her side, and read over her shoulder.

She turned to him. "Don't you have anything to do?"

"Giles and Keja say I keep getting in the way," he answered with a frown. "Sometimes I don't like them very much."

"They have much to do before we leave Shahal," Petia said. "It's too bad you can't read, Anji. I can use some help."

"Will you teach me to read someday? Can I watch?"

"Of course, but you must be quiet, please. I've got to find some way to free Djinn from his spell." She concentrated on the words.

The letters on the page fascinated Anji. Petia had told him that the letters made words, and he knew that words had meaning. Still, he did not understand it. He studied the illuminations of the capital letters and the illustrations that appeared at the top of some pages. Some were gory and others had been drawn by someone with a sense of humor.

Petia reached to turn a page when something caught Anji's attention. "Wait," he cried.

"What is it?" she said, concerned that he had seen something that upset him.

He pointed to the illustration at the top of the left-hand page. "That's not our Djinn, but it's like the djinn in the stories I heard when I was little."

Petia laughed. "You're still little," she said, tousling his hair.

"But it is, Mistress," the boy pleaded. He pointed again at the drawing. "See, the muscles in his arms and the scimitar pointing. And he's wearing a vest, but no tunic underneath. And baggy pants. It's a djinn, like in the stories. And maybe that is the page for the spell."

Petia examined the page once more, reading the title at

the top of the page slowly. "For making the eyes of an enemy weep as if there were grains of sand in them." She shook her head. "It has nothing to do with djinn."

Crestfallen, the boy scowled. "That's a djinn," he insisted. "I know a picture of a djinn when I see one." He crossed his arms in disgust. "What's he pointing his scimitar at?"

Petia looked back at the figure. The djinn did hold his scimitar as if pointing. She followed the direction across the page, but nothing unusual appeared on the right-hand page. She read the title once more. Its meaning was veiled. At the top, in tiny printing by another hand, a one-word warning read: "Cautiously!"

She studied the title, puzzled about the meaning: "For XXXXX."

In a flash of inspiration, it became clear to her. She looked at the bottom of the page. A shaft with spearheads pointing both directions gave her the clue. The spell recited backwards would undo whatever it had done in the first place. She began to read the words softly to herself, then realized that she might accidentally turn Anji into a djinn.

When she had finished reading, Petia felt uncertain that it was the correct spell. The word "djinn" did not appear in the spell, but references to a being who would serve, who would do one's bidding, were abundant. She sucked in her breath. There was only one way to find out if this would work.

"Djinn, are you here?" she called.

The spirit materialized and glared at her. "What do you want?" he said sullenly.

"I think I have the spell of unbinding." She almost laughed at the change of expression on his face. She explained that she was willing to try the unknown spell, but the final decision had to rest on Djinn's shoulders.

"I'll try every spell in every book," he promised.

"No, you won't. Unless you want to be changed into something worse than a djinn. Now compose yourself."

Petia took a deep breath and tried to follow her own advice. She said the words evenly, maintaining a calm. Afraid to look up at Djinn, fearing that the spell would not work, she concentrated on the words.

As she finished the last word, she closed her eyes. She felt hands pulling her up from the bench and nearly panicked.

Arms swirled Petia off her feet, and she found herself being danced around the room by a handsome young man.

"You did it, you did it!" The young man, so much like Djinn but not the spirit, set Petia down, hugged her, then dabbed at his eyes.

Anji tugged at his arm. "Is that you, Djinn?"

"Yes, no. I mean, yes, I was Djinn, but now I'm me. I'm again Hassan, Prince of the Mullaheed Harifim!"

"I'm so pleased, Djinn—Hassan," Petia said. "I didn't want to give up, but I was getting discouraged."

Word spread through Shahal, and soon another celebration was under way that lasted long into the night. By the time it ended and everyone staggered off to bed, a pact between Hassan and the beasts had been made. He would stay in Shahal and act as a mediator between the beasts and the Harifim.

The humans and Trans began serious preparations for leaving. The two Harifim who had been sent back to the tribes reappeared and conferred at great length with Hassan. The first steps toward a lasting truce between desert clans and the beasts had been taken, and Hassan delivered to Giles five strong desert steeds as payment for all they'd done.

"It's time for us to leave," Giles said to Petia and Keja. "The beasts are caught up in repairing Shahal, and the Harifim brought horses for us. We've no excuse to stay now. We'll head south and find a ship there. There's no sense going back to Kasha and asking for trouble."

Petia boosted Anji up into his saddle. The boy leaned forward and whispered into the horse's ear. It flicked in understanding.

Hassan came to Petia and folded her hands in his, then bowed until his forehead touched her hands. "Thank you, good lady. I'll always remember you." She blushed.

Hassan clasped hands with Giles and Keja, then stepped back. He watched them mount and ride off into the fading light. "May the gods guide you and keep you safe," he called after them. Red Mane and the other beasts silently watched as they put the spurs to their mounts.

Giles laughed and let the wind rush past his face. Freedom! He cried, "To Khelora!" and the others joined him in the chant.

From the clifftop behind Shahal, a man robed in black threw his hood back. On his left wrist, a large hawk pranced in anticipation. He watched the five horses separate from the Harifim encampment near Shahal and proceed toward a defile in the hills to the south.

"Good, very good," he said softly. "Four keys they have now. And I hold the fifth. The Gate of Paradise will open soon—for me!" Mocking laughter drifted across the desert and, swallowed by distance, died.